Of Ghosts and Goblins

Lafcadio Hearn

Of Ghosts and Goblins

PENGUIN CLASSICS
an imprint of
PENGUIN BOOKS

PENGUIN CLASSICS

UK | USA | Canada | Ireland | Australia
India | New Zealand | South Africa

Penguin Books is part of the Penguin Random House group of companies
whose addresses can be found at global.penguinrandomhouse.com.

Stories first published 1894–1905. This selection is taken
from *Japanese Ghost Stories*, Penguin Classics 2019.
'Of Ghosts and Goblins' is an extract from a longer chapter with
the same title; all footnotes are authorial.
Published in Little Clothbound Classics 2022.

002

Cover design and illustration by Coralie Bickford-Smith

Set in 9.5/13pt Baskerville 10 Pro
Typeset by Jouve (UK), Milton Keynes
Printed and bound in Great Britain by Clays Ltd, Elcograf S.p.A.

The authorized representative in the EEA is Penguin Random House Ireland,
Morrison Chambers, 32 Nassau Street, Dublin D02 YH68

A CIP catalogue record for this book is available from the British Library

ISBN: 978-0-241-57372-3

Contents

Contents

Of Ghosts and Goblins

A long time ago, in the days when Fox-women and goblins haunted this land, there came to the capital with her parents a samurai girl, so beautiful that all men who saw her fell enamored of her. And hundreds of young samurai desired and hoped to marry her, and made their desire known to her parents. For it has ever been the custom in Japan that marriages should be arranged by parents. But there are exceptions to all customs, and the case of this maiden was such an exception. Her parents declared that they intended to allow their daughter to choose her own husband, and that all who wished to win her would be free to woo her.

Many men of high rank and of great wealth were admitted to the house as suitors; and each one courted her as he best knew how – with gifts, and with fair words, and with poems written in her honor, and with promises of eternal love. And to each one she spoke sweetly and hopefully; but she made strange conditions. For every suitor she obliged to bind himself by his word of honor as a samurai to submit to a test of his love for her, and never to divulge to living person what that test might be. And to this all agreed.

But even the most confident suitors suddenly ceased

their importunities after having been put to the test; and all of them appeared to have been greatly terrified by something. Indeed, not a few even fled away from the city, and could not be persuaded by their friends to return. But no one ever so much as hinted why. Therefore it was whispered by those who knew nothing of the mystery, that the beautiful girl must be either a Fox-woman or a goblin.

Now, when all the wooers of high rank had abandoned their suit, there came a samurai who had no wealth but his sword. He was a good man and true, and of pleasing presence; and the girl seemed to like him. But she made him take the same pledge which the others had taken; and after he had taken it, she told him to return upon a certain evening.

When that evening came, he was received at the house by none but the girl herself. With her own hands she set before him the repast of hospitality, and waited upon him, after which she told him that she wished him to go out with her at a late hour. To this he consented gladly, and inquired to what place she desired to go. But she replied nothing to his question, and all at once became very silent, and strange in her manner. And after a while she retired from the apartment, leaving him alone.

Only long after midnight she returned, robed all in white – like a Soul – and, without uttering a word, signed to him to follow her. Out of the house they hastened while all the city slept. It was what is called an *oborozuki-yo* – 'moon-clouded night'. Always upon such a night, 'tis said, do ghosts wander. She swiftly led the way; and the dogs howled as she flitted by; and she passed beyond the confines of the city to a place of knolls shadowed by enormous trees, where an ancient cemetery was. Into it she glided – a white shadow into blackness. He followed, wondering, his hand upon his sword. Then his eyes became accustomed to the gloom; and he saw.

By a new-made grave she paused and signed to him to wait. The tools of the grave-maker were still lying there. Seizing one, she began to dig furiously, with strange haste and strength. At last her spade smote a coffin-lid and made it boom: another moment and the fresh white wood of the *kwan* was bare. She tore off the lid, revealing a corpse within – the corpse of a child. With goblin gestures she wrung an arm from the body, wrenched it in twain, and, squatting down, began to devour the upper half. Then, flinging to her lover the other half, she cried to him, *'Eat, if thou lovest me! this is what I eat!'*

Not even for a single instant did he hesitate. He squatted down upon the other side of the grave, and ate the half of the arm, and said, *'Kekkō degozarimasu! mo sukoshi chōdai.'** For that arm was made of the best *kwashi*† that Saikyō could produce.

---

* 'It is excellent: I pray you give me a little more.'
† *Kwashi*: Japanese confectionery.

Then the girl sprang to her feet with a burst of laughter, and cried: 'You only, of all my brave suitors, did not run away! And I wanted a husband who could not fear. I will marry you; I can love you: you are *a man!*'

The Dream of a Summer Day

I

The hotel seemed to me a paradise, and the maids thereof celestial beings. This was because I had just fled away from one of the Open Ports, where I had ventured to seek comfort in a European hotel, supplied with all 'modern improvements'. To find myself at ease once more in a *yukata*, seated upon cool, soft matting, waited upon by sweet-voiced girls, and surrounded by things of beauty, was therefore like a redemption from all the sorrows of the nineteenth century. Bamboo-shoots and lotus-bulbs were given me for breakfast, and a fan from heaven for a keepsake. The design upon that fan represented only the white rushing burst of one great wave on a beach, and sea-birds shooting in exultation through the blue over-head. But to behold it was worth all the trouble of the journey. It was a glory of light, a thunder of motion, a triumph of sea-wind – all in one. It made me want to shout when I looked at it.

Between the cedarn balcony pillars I could see the course of the pretty gray town following the shore-sweep – and yellow lazy junks asleep at anchor – and the opening of the bay between enormous green cliffs – and beyond it the blaze of summer to the horizon. In that horizon there were mountain shapes faint as old memories. And all things but the gray town, and the yellow junks, and the green cliffs, were blue.

Then a voice softly toned as a wind-bell began to tinkle words of courtesy into my reverie, and broke it; and I perceived that the mistress of the palace had come to thank me for the *chadai*,* and I prostrated myself before her. She was very young, and more than pleasant to look upon – like the moth maidens, like the butterfly-women, of Kunisada. And I thought at once of death; for the beautiful is sometimes a sorrow of anticipation.

She asked whither I honorably intended to go, that she might order a *kuruma* for me.

And I made answer:

'To Kumamoto. But the name of your house I much wish to know, that I may always remember it.'

'My guest-rooms,' she said, 'are augustly insignificant, and my maidens honorably rude. But the house is called the House of Urashima. And now I go to order a *kuruma*.'

The music of her voice passed; and I felt enchantment falling all about me – like the thrilling of a ghostly web.

---

* A little gift of money, always made to a hotel by the guest shortly after his arrival.

For the name was the name of the story of a song that bewitches men.

II

Once you hear the story, you will never be able to forget it. Every summer when I find myself on the coast – especially of very soft, still days – it haunts me most persistently. There are many native versions of it which have been the inspiration for countless works of art. But the most impressive and the most ancient is found in the 'Manye-fushifu', a collection of poems dating from the fifth to the ninth century. From this ancient version the great scholar Aston translated it into prose, and the great scholar Chamberlain into both prose and verse. But for English readers I think the most charming form of it is Chamberlain's version written for children, in the 'Japa-nese Fairy-Tale Series' – because of the delicious colored pictures by native artists. With that little book before me, I shall try to tell the legend over again in my own words.

Fourteen hundred and sixteen years ago, the fisher-boy Urashima Tarō left the shore of Suminoyé in his boat.

Summer days were then as now – all drowsy and ten-der blue, with only some light, pure white clouds hanging over the mirror of the sea. Then, too, were the hills the same – far blue soft shapes melting into the blue sky. And the winds were lazy.

And presently the boy, also lazy, let his boat drift as he fished. It was a queer boat, unpainted and rudderless, of a shape you probably never saw. But still, after fourteen hundred years, there are such boats to be seen in front of the ancient fishing-hamlets of the coast of the Sea of Japan.

After long waiting, Urashima caught something, and drew it up to him. But he found it was only a tortoise.

Now a tortoise is sacred to the Dragon God of the Sea, and the period of its natural life is a thousand – some say ten thousand – years. So that to kill it is very wrong. The boy gently unfastened the creature from his line, and set it free, with a prayer to the gods.

But he caught nothing more. And the day was very warm; and sea and air and all things were very, very silent. And a great drowsiness grew upon him – and he slept in his drifting boat.

Then out of the dreaming of the sea rose up a beautiful girl – just as you can see her in the picture to Professor Chamberlain's 'Urashima' – robed in crimson and blue, with long black hair flowing down her back even to her feet, after the fashion of a prince's daughter fourteen hundred years ago.

Gliding over the waters she came, softly as air; and she stood above the sleeping boy in the boat, and woke him with a light touch, and said:

'Do not be surprised. My father, the Dragon King of the Sea, sent me to you, because of your kind heart. For to-day you set free a tortoise. And now we will go to my father's palace in the island where summer never dies; and I will be your flower-wife if you wish; and we shall live there happily forever.'

And Urashima wondered more and more as he looked upon her; for she was more beautiful than any human being, and he could not but love her. Then she took one oar, and he took another, and they rowed away together – just as you may still see, off the far western coast, wife and husband rowing together, when the fishing-boats flit into the evening gold.

They rowed away softly and swiftly over the silent blue water down into the south – till they came to the island where summer never dies – and to the palace of the Dragon King of the Sea.

[Here the text of the little book suddenly shrinks away as you read, and faint blue ripplings flood the page; and beyond them in a fairy horizon you can see the long low soft shore of the island, and peaked roofs rising through evergreen foliage – the roofs of the Sea God's palace – like the palace of the Mikado Yuriaku, fourteen hundred and sixteen years ago.]

There strange servitors came to receive them in robes of ceremony – creatures of the Sea, who paid greeting to Urashima as the son-in-law of the Dragon King.

So the Sea God's daughter became the bride of

9

Urashima; and it was a bridal of wondrous splendor; and in the Dragon Palace there was great rejoicing.

And each day for Urashima there were new wonders and new pleasures: wonders of the deepest deep brought up by the servants of the Ocean God; pleasures of that enchanted land where summer never dies. And so three years passed.

But in spite of all these things, the fisher-boy felt always a heaviness at his heart when he thought of his parents waiting alone. So that at last he prayed his bride to let him go home for a little while only, just to say one word to his father and mother – after which he would hasten back to her.

At these words she began to weep; and for a long time she continued to weep silently. Then she said to him: 'Since you wish to go, of course you must go. I fear your going very much; I fear we shall never see each other again. But I will give you a little box to take with you. It will help you to come back to me if you will do what I tell you. Do not open it. Above all things, do not open it – no matter what may happen! Because, if you open it, you will never be able to come back, and you will never see me again.'

Then she gave him a little lacquered box tied about with a silken cord. [And that box can be seen unto this day in the temple of Kanagawa, by the seashore; and the priests there also keep Urashima Tarō's fishing line, and some strange jewels which he brought back with him from the realm of the Dragon King.]

But Urashima comforted his bride, and promised her never, never to open the box – never even to loosen the silken string. Then he passed away through the summer light over the ever-sleeping sea; and the shape of the island where summer never dies faded behind him like a dream; and he saw again before him the blue mountains of Japan, sharpening in the white glow of the northern horizon.

Again at last he glided into his native bay; again he stood upon its beach. But as he looked, there came upon him a great bewilderment – a weird doubt.

For the place was at once the same, and yet not the same. The cottage of his fathers had disappeared. There was a village; but the shapes of the houses were all strange, and the trees were strange, and the fields, and even the faces of the people. Nearly all remembered landmarks were gone; the Shintō temple appeared to have been rebuilt in a new place; the woods had vanished from the neighboring slopes. Only the voice of the little stream flowing through the settlement, and the forms of the mountains, were still the same. All else was unfamiliar and new. In vain he tried to find the dwelling of his parents; and the fisherfolk stared wonderingly at him; and he could not remember having ever seen any of those faces before.

There came along a very old man, leaning on a stick, and Urashima asked him the way to the house of the Urashima family. But the old man looked quite astonished, and made him repeat the question many times, and then cried out:

'Urashima Tarō! Where do you come from that you do not know the story? Urashima Tarō! Why, it is more than four hundred years since he was drowned, and a monument is erected to his memory in the graveyard. The graves of all his people are in that graveyard – the old graveyard which is not now used any more. Urashima Tarō! How can you be so foolish as to ask where his house is?' And the old man hobbled on, laughing at the simplicity of his questioner.

But Urashima went to the village graveyard – the old graveyard that was not used any more – and there he found his own tombstone, and the tombstones of his father and his mother and his kindred, and the tombstones of many others he had known. So old they were, so moss-eaten, that it was very hard to read the names upon them.

Then he knew himself the victim of some strange illusion, and he took his way back to the beach – always carrying in his hand the box, the gift of the Sea God's daughter. But what was this illusion? And what could be in that box? Or might not that which was in the box be the cause of the illusion? Doubt mastered faith. Recklessly he broke the promise made to his beloved; he loosened the silken cord; he opened the box!

Instantly, without any sound, there burst from it a white cold spectral vapor that rose in air like a summer cloud, and began to drift away swiftly into the south, over the silent sea. There was nothing else in the box.

And Urashima then knew that he had destroyed his own happiness – that he could never again return to his beloved, the daughter of the Ocean King. So that he wept and cried out bitterly in his despair.

Yet for a moment only. In another, he himself was changed. An icy chill shot through all his blood; his teeth fell out; his face shriveled; his hair turned white as snow; his limbs withered; his strength ebbed; he sank down lifeless on the sand, crushed by the weight of four hundred winters.

Now in the official annals of the Emperors it is written that 'in the twenty-first year of the Mikado Yuriaku, the boy Urashima of Midzunoyé, in the district of Yosa, in the province of Tango, a descendant of the divinity Shimanemi, went to Elysium [*Hōrai*] in a fishing-boat.' After this there is no more news of Urashima during the reigns of thirty-one emperors and empresses – that is, from the fifth until the ninth century. And then the annals announce that 'in the second year of Tenchiyō, in the reign of the Mikado Go-Junwa, the boy Urashima returned, and presently departed again, none knew whither.'*

---

* See *The Classical Poetry of the Japanese*, by Professor Chamberlain, in Trübner's Oriental Series. According to Western chronology, Urashima went fishing in 477 AD, and returned in 825.

III

The fairy mistress came back to tell me that everything was ready, and tried to lift my valise in her slender hands – which I prevented her from doing, because it was heavy. Then she laughed, but would not suffer that I should carry it myself, and summoned a sea-creature with Chinese characters upon his back. I made obeisance to her; and she prayed me to remember the unworthy house despite the rudeness of the maidens. 'And you will pay the *kurumaya*,' she said, 'only seventy-five sen.'

Then I slipped into the vehicle; and in a few minutes the little gray town had vanished behind a curve. I was rolling along a white road overlooking the shore. To the right were pale brown cliffs; to the left only space and sea.

Mile after mile I rolled along that shore, looking into the infinite light. All was steeped in blue – a marvelous blue, like that which comes and goes in the heart of a great shell. Glowing blue sea met hollow blue sky in a brightness of electric fusion; and vast blue apparitions – the mountains of Higo – angled up through the blaze, like masses of amethyst. What a blue transparency! The universal color was broken only by the dazzling white of a few high summer clouds, motionlessly curled above one phantom peak in the offing. They threw down upon the water snowy tremulous lights. Midges of ships creeping far away seemed to pull long threads after them – the only sharp lines in all that hazy glory. But what divine clouds! White purified spirits of clouds, resting on their way to the beatitude of Nirvana? Or perhaps the mists escaped from Urashima's box a thousand years ago?

The gnat of the soul of me flitted out into that dream of blue, 'twixt sea and sun – hummed back to the shore of Suminoyé through the luminous ghosts of fourteen hundred summers. Vaguely I felt beneath me the drifting of a keel. It was the time of the Mikado Yuriaku. And the Daughter of the Dragon King said tinklingly, 'Now we will go to my father's palace where it is always blue.' 'Why always blue?' I asked. 'Because,' she said, 'I put all the clouds into the Box.' 'But I must go home,' I answered resolutely. 'Then,' she said, 'you will pay the *kurumaya* only seventy-five sen.'

Wherewith I woke into Doyō, or the Period of Greatest Heat, in the twenty-sixth year of Meiji – and saw proof of the era in a line of telegraph poles reaching out of sight on the land side of the way. The *kuruma* was still fleeing by the shore, before the same blue vision of sky, peak, and sea; but the white clouds were gone! – and there were no more cliffs close to the road, but fields of rice and of

15

barley stretching to far-off hills. The telegraph lines absorbed my attention for a moment, because on the top wire, and only on the top wire, hosts of little birds were perched, all with their heads to the road, and nowise disturbed by our coming. They remained quite still, looking down upon us as mere passing phenomena. There were hundreds and hundreds in rank, for miles and miles. And I could not see one having its tail turned to the road. Why they sat thus, and what they were watching or waiting for, I could not guess. At intervals I waved my hat and shouted, to startle the ranks. Whereupon a few would rise up fluttering and chippering, and drop back again upon the wire in the same position as before. The vast majority refused to take me seriously.

The sharp rattle of the wheels was drowned by a deep booming; and as we whirled past a village I caught sight of an immense drum under an open shed, beaten by naked men.

'O *kurumaya*!' I shouted – 'that – what is it?'

He, without stopping, shouted back:

'Everywhere now the same thing is. Much time-in rain has not been: so the gods-to prayers are made, and drums are beaten.'

We flashed through other villages; and I saw and heard more drums of various sizes, and from hamlets invisible, over miles of parching rice-fields, yet other drums, like echoings, responded.

IV

Then I began to think about Urashima again. I thought of the pictures and poems and proverbs recording the influence of the legend upon the imagination of a race. I thought of an Izumo dancing-girl I saw at a banquet acting the part of Urashima, with a little lacquered box whence there issued at the tragical minute a mist of Kyōto incense. I thought about the antiquity of the beautiful dance – and therefore about vanished generations of dancing-girls – and therefore about dust in the abstract; which, again, led me to think of dust in the concrete, as bestirred by the sandals of the *kurumaya* to whom I was to pay only seventy-five sen. And I wondered how much of it might be old human dust, and whether in the eternal order of things the motion of hearts might be of more consequence than the motion of dust. Then my ancestral morality took alarm; and I tried to persuade myself that a story which had lived for a thousand years, gaining fresher charm with the passing of every century, could only have survived by virtue of some truth in it. But what truth? For the time being I could find no answer to this question.

The heat had become very great; and I cried,

'O *kurumaya*! the throat of Selfishness is dry; water desirable is.'

He, still running, answered:

'The Village of the Long Beach inside of – not far – a great gush-water is. There pure august water will be given.'

I cried again:

'O *kurumaya*! – those little birds as-for, why this way always facing?'

He, running still more swiftly, responded:

'All birds wind-to facing sit.'

I laughed first at my own simplicity; then at my forgetfulness – remembering I had been told the same thing, somewhere or other, when a boy. Perhaps the mystery of Urashima might also have been created by forgetfulness.

I thought again about Urashima. I saw the Daughter of the Dragon King waiting vainly in the palace made beautiful for his welcome – and the pitiless return of the Cloud, announcing what had happened – and the loving uncouth sea-creatures, in their garments of great ceremony, trying to comfort her. But in the real story there was nothing of all this; and the pity of the people seemed to be all for Urashima. And I began to discourse with myself thus:

Is it right to pity Urashima at all? Of course he was bewildered by the gods. But who is not bewildered by the gods? What is Life itself but a bewilderment? And Urashima in his bewilderment doubted the purpose of the gods, and opened the box. Then he died without any trouble, and the people built a shrine to him as Urashima Miō-jin. Why, then, so much pity?

Things are quite differently managed in the West. After disobeying Western gods, we have still to remain alive and to learn the height and the breadth and the depth of superlative sorrow. We are not allowed to die quite comfortably just at the best possible time: much less are we suffered to become after death small gods in our own right. How can we pity the folly of Urashima after he had lived so long alone with visible gods.

Perhaps the fact that we do may answer the riddle. This pity must be self-pity; wherefore the legend may be the legend of a myriad souls. The thought of it comes just at a particular time of blue light and soft wind – and always like an old reproach. It has too intimate relation to a season and the feeling of a season not to be also related to something real in one's life, or in the lives of one's ancestors. But what was that real something? Who was the Daughter of the Dragon King? Where was the island of unending summer? And what was the cloud in the box?

I cannot answer all those questions. I know this only – which is not at all new:

I have memory of a place and a magical time in which the Sun and the Moon were larger and brighter than now. Whether it was of this life or of some life before I cannot tell. But I know the sky was very much more blue, and nearer to the world – almost as it seems to become above the masts of a steamer steaming into equatorial summer. The sea was alive, and used to talk – and the Wind made me cry out for joy when it touched me. Once or twice during other years, in divine days lived among the peaks, I have dreamed just for a moment that the same wind was blowing – but it was only a remembrance.

Also in that place the clouds were wonderful, and of colors for which there are no names at all – colors that used to make me hungry and thirsty. I remember, too, that the days were ever so much longer than these days – and that every day there were new wonders and new pleasures for me. And all that country and time were softly ruled by One who thought only of ways to make me happy. Sometimes I would refuse to be made happy, and that always caused her pain, although she was divine; and I remember that I tried very hard to be sorry. When day was done, and there fell the great hush of the light before moonrise, she would tell me stories that made me tingle from head to foot with pleasure. I have never heard any other stories half so beautiful. And when the pleasure became too great, she would sing a weird little song which always brought sleep. At last there came a parting day; and she wept, and told me of a charm she had given that I must never, never lose, because it would keep me young, and give me power to return. But I never returned. And the years went; and one day I knew that I had lost the charm, and had become ridiculously old.

V

The Village of the Long Beach is at the foot of a green cliff near the road, and consists of a dozen thatched cottages clustered about a rocky pool, shaded by pines. The basin overflows with cold water, supplied by a stream that leaps straight from the heart of the cliff – just as folks imagine that a poem ought to spring straight from the heart of a poet. It was evidently a favorite halting-place, judging by the number of *kuruma* and of people resting. There were benches under the trees; and, after having allayed thirst, I sat down to smoke and to look at the women washing clothes and the travelers refreshing themselves at the pool – while my *kurumaya* stripped, and proceeded to dash buckets of cold water over his body. Then tea was brought me by a young man with a baby on his back; and I tried to play with the baby, which said 'Ah, bah!'

Such are the first sounds uttered by a Japanese babe. But they are purely Oriental; and in Romaji should be written *Aba*. And, as an utterance untaught, *Aba* is interesting. It is in Japanese child-speech the word for 'good-bye' – precisely the last we would expect an infant to pronounce on entering into this world of illusion. To whom or to what is the little soul saying good-bye? – to friends in a previous state of existence still freshly remembered? – to comrades of its shadowy journey from nobody-knows-where? Such theorizing is tolerably safe, from a pious point of view, since the child can never decide for us. What its thoughts were at that mysterious moment of first speech, it will have forgotten long before it has become able to answer questions.

Unexpectedly, a queer recollection came to me – resurrected, perhaps, by the sight of the young man with the baby – perhaps by the song of the water in the cliff; the recollection of a story:

Long, long ago there lived somewhere among the mountains a poor woodcutter and his wife. They were very old, and had no children. Every day the husband went alone to the forest to cut wood, while the wife sat weaving at home.

One day the old man went farther into the forest than was his custom, to seek a certain kind of wood; and he suddenly found himself at the edge of a little spring he had never seen before. The water was strangely clear and cold, and he was thirsty; for the day was hot, and he had been working hard. So he doffed his great straw hat, knelt down, and took a long drink. That water seemed to refresh him in a most extraordinary way. Then he caught sight of his own face in the spring, and started back. It was certainly his own face, but not at all as he was accustomed to see it in the old mirror at home. It was the face of a very young man! He could not believe his eyes. He put up both hands to his head, which had been quite bald only a moment before. It was covered with thick black hair. And his face had become smooth as a boy's; every wrinkle was gone. At the same moment he discovered himself full of new strength. He stared in astonishment at the limbs that had been so long withered by age; they were now shapely and hard with dense young muscle. Unknowingly he had drunk at the Fountain of Youth; and that draught had transformed him.

First, he leaped high and shouted for joy; then he ran home faster than he had ever run before in his life. When he entered his house his wife was frightened – because she took him for a stranger; and when he told her the wonder, she could not at once believe him. But after a long time he was able to convince her that the young man she now saw before her was really her husband; and he told her where the spring was, and asked her to go there with him.

Then she said: 'You have become so handsome and so young that you cannot continue to love an old woman; so I must drink some of that water immediately. But it will never do for both of us to be away from the house at the same time. Do you wait here while I go.' And she ran to the woods all by herself.

She found the spring and knelt down, and began to drink. Oh! how cool and sweet that water was! She drank and drank and drank, and stopped for breath only to begin again.

Her husband waited for her impatiently; he expected to see her come back changed into a pretty slender girl.

But she did not come back at all. He got anxious, shut up the house, and went to look for her.

When he reached the spring, he could not see her. He was just on the point of returning when he heard a little wail in the high grass near the spring. He searched there and discovered his wife's clothes and a baby – a very small baby, perhaps six months old!

For the old woman had drunk too deeply of the magical water; she had drunk herself far back beyond the time of youth into the period of speechless infancy.

He took up the child in his arms. It looked at him in a sad, wondering way. He carried it home – murmuring to it – thinking strange, melancholy thoughts.

In that hour, after my reverie about Urashima, the moral of this story seemed less satisfactory than in former time. Because by drinking too deeply of life we do not become young.

Naked and cool my *kurumaya* returned, and said that because of the heat he could not finish the promised run of twenty-five miles, but that he had found another runner to take me the rest of the way. For so much as he himself had done, he wanted fifty-five sen.

It was really very hot – more than 100° I afterwards learned; and far away there throbbed continually, like a pulsation of the heat itself, the sound of great drums beating for rain. And I thought of the Daughter of the Dragon King.

'Seventy-five sen, she told me,' I observed; 'and that promised to be done has not been done. Nevertheless, seventy-five sen to you shall be given – because I am afraid of the gods.'

And behind a yet unwearied runner I fled away into the enormous blaze – in the direction of the great drums.

The Eternal Haunter

This year the Tōkyō color-prints – *Nishiki-é* – seem to me of unusual interest. They reproduce, or almost reproduce, the color-charm of the early broadsides; and they show a marked improvement in line-drawing. Certainly one could not wish for anything prettier than the best prints of the present season.

My latest purchase has been a set of weird studies – spectres of all kinds known to the Far East, including many varieties not yet discovered in the West. Some are extremely unpleasant; but a few are really charming. Here, for example, is a delicious thing by 'Chikanobu', just published, and for sale at the remarkable price of three sen!

Can you guess what it represents? . . . Yes, a girl, but what kind of a girl? Study it a little . . . Very lovely, is she not, with that shy sweetness in her downcast gaze – that light and dainty grace, as of a resting butterfly? . . . No, she is not some Psyche of the most Eastern East, in the sense that you mean – but she is a soul. Observe that the cherry-flowers falling from the branch above, are passing *through* her form. See also the folds of her robe, below, melting into blue faint mist. How delicate and vapory the whole thing is! It gives you the feeling of spring; and all those fairy colors are the colors of a Japanese spring-morning . . . No, she is not the personification of any season. Rather she is a dream – such a dream as might haunt the slumbers of Far-Eastern youth; but the artist did not intend her to represent a dream . . . You cannot guess? Well, she is a tree-spirit – the Spirit of the Cherry-tree. Only in the twilight of morning or of evening she appears, gliding about her tree; and whoever sees her must love her. But, if approached, she vanishes back into the trunk, like a vapor absorbed. There is a legend of one tree-spirit who loved a man, and even gave him a son; but such conduct was quite at variance with the shy habits of her race . . .

You ask what is the use of drawing the Impossible? Your asking proves that you do not feel the charm of this vision of youth – this dream of spring. *I* hold that the Impossible bears a much closer relation to fact than does most of what we call the real and the commonplace. The Impossible may not be naked truth; but I think that it is usually truth – masked and veiled, perhaps, but eternal. Now to me this Japanese dream is true – true, at least, as human love is. Considered even as a ghost it is true. Whoever pretends not to believe in ghosts of any sort, lies to his own heart. Every man is haunted by ghosts. And this color-print reminds me of a ghost whom we all know – though most of us (poets excepted) are unwilling to confess the acquaintance.

*

Perhaps – for it happens to some of us – you may have seen this haunter, in dreams of the night, even during childhood. Then, of course, you could not know the beautiful shape bending above your rest: possibly you thought her to be an angel, or the soul of a dead sister. But in waking life we first become aware of her presence about the time when boyhood begins to ripen into youth.

This first of her apparitions is a shock of ecstasy, a breathless delight; but the wonder and the pleasure are quickly followed by a sense of sadness inexpressible – totally unlike any sadness ever felt before – though in her gaze there is only caress, and on her lips the most exquisite of smiles. And you cannot imagine the reason of that feeling until you have learned who she is – which is not an easy thing to learn.

Only a moment she remains; but during that luminous moment all the tides of your being set and surge to her with a longing for which there is not any word. And then – suddenly! – she is not; and you find that the sun has gloomed, the colors of the world turned gray.

Thereafter enchantment remains between you and all that you loved before – persons or things or places. None of them will ever seem again so near and dear as in other days.

Often she will return. Once that you have seen her she will never cease to visit you. And this haunting – ineffably sweet, inexplicably sad – may fill you with rash desire to wander over the world in search of somebody like her.

But however long and far you wander, never will you find that somebody.

Later you may learn to fear her visits because of the pain they bring – the strange pain that you cannot understand. But the breadth of zones and seas cannot divide you from her; walls of iron cannot exclude her. Soundless and subtle as a shudder of ether is the motion of her.

Ancient her beauty as the heart of man – yet ever waxing fairer, forever remaining young. Mortals wither in Time as leaves in the frost of autumn; but Time only brightens the glow and the bloom of her endless youth.

All men have loved her; all must continue to love her. But none shall touch with his lips even the hem of her garment.

All men adore her; yet all she deceives, and many are the ways of her deception. Most often she lures her lover into the presence of some earthly maid, and blends herself incomprehensibly with the body of that maid, and works such sudden glamour that the human gaze becomes divine – that the human limbs shine through their raiment. But presently the luminous haunter detaches herself from the mortal, and leaves her dupe to wonder at the mockery of sense.

No man can describe her, though nearly all men have some time tried to do so. Pictured she cannot be – since her beauty itself is a ceaseless becoming, multiple to infinitude, and tremulous with perpetual quickening, as with flowing of light.

There is a story, indeed, that thousands of years ago some marvellous sculptor was able to fix in stone a single remembrance of her. But this doing became for many the cause of sorrow supreme; and the Gods decreed, out of compassion, that to no other mortal should ever be given power to work the like wonder. In these years we can worship only; we cannot portray.

But who is she? – what is she? . . . Ah! that is what I wanted you to ask. Well, she has never had a name; but I shall call her a tree-spirit.

The Japanese say that you can exorcise a tree-spirit – if you are cruel enough to do it – simply by cutting down her tree.

But you cannot exorcise the Spirit of whom I speak – nor ever cut down her tree.

For her tree is the measureless, timeless, billion-branching Tree of Life – even the World-Tree, Yggdrasil, whose roots are in Night and Death, whose head is above the Gods.

Seek to woo her – she is Echo. Seek to clasp her – she is Shadow. But her smile will haunt you into the hour of dissolution and beyond – through numberless lives to come.

And never will you return her smile – never, because of that which it awakens within you – the pain that you cannot understand.

And never, never shall you win to her – because she is the phantom light of long-expired suns – because she was shaped by the beating of infinite millions of hearts that are dust – because her witchery was made in the endless ebb and flow of the visions and hopes of youth, through countless forgotten cycles of your own incalculable past.

Fragment

And it was at the hour of sunset that they came to the foot of the mountain. There was in that place no sign of life – neither token of water, nor trace of plant, nor shadow of flying bird – nothing but desolation rising to desolation. And the summit was lost in heaven.

Then the Bodhisattva said to his young companion: 'What you have asked to see will be shown to you. But the place of the Vision is far; and the way is rude. Follow after me, and do not fear: strength will be given you.'

Twilight gloomed about them as they climbed. There was no beaten path, nor any mark of former human visitation; and the way was over an endless heaping of tumbled fragments that rolled or turned beneath the foot. Sometimes a mass dislodged would clatter down with hollow echoings; sometimes the substance trodden would burst like an empty shell ... Stars pointed and thrilled; and the darkness deepened.

'Do not fear, my son,' said the Bodhisattva, guiding: 'danger there is none, though the way be grim.'

Under the stars they climbed – fast, fast – mounting

by help of power superhuman. High zones of mist they passed; and they saw below them, ever widening as they climbed, a soundless flood of cloud, like the tide of a milky sea.

Hour after hour they climbed; and forms invisible yielded to their tread with dull soft crashings; and faint cold fires lighted and died at every breaking.

And once the pilgrim-youth laid hand on a something smooth that was not stone – and lifted it – and dimly saw the cheekless gibe of death.

'Linger not thus, my son!' urged the voice of the teacher; 'the summit that we must gain is very far away!'

On through the dark they climbed – and felt continually beneath them the soft strange breakings – and saw the icy fires worm and die – till the rim of the night turned gray, and the stars began to fail, and the east began to bloom.

Yet still they climbed – fast, fast – mounting by help of power superhuman. About them now was frigidness of death – and silence tremendous . . . A gold flame kindled in the east.

Then first to the pilgrim's gaze the steeps revealed their nakedness; and a trembling seized him – and a ghastly fear. For there was not any ground – neither beneath him nor about him nor above him – but a heaping only, monstrous and measureless, of skulls and fragments of skulls and dust of bone – with a shimmer of shed teeth strown through the drift of it, like the shimmer of scrags of shell in the wrack of a tide.

'Do not fear, my son!' cried the voice of the Bodhisattva; 'only the strong of heart can win to the place of the Vision!'

Behind them the world had vanished. Nothing remained but the clouds beneath, and the sky above, and the heaping of skulls between – upslanting out of sight.

Then the sun climbed with the climbers; and there was no warmth in the light of him, but coldness sharp as a sword. And the horror of stupendous height, and the nightmare of stupendous depth, and the terror of silence, ever grew and grew, and weighed upon the pilgrim, and held his feet – so that suddenly all power departed from him, and he moaned like a sleeper in dreams.

'Hasten, hasten, my son!' cried the Bodhisattva: 'the day is brief, and the summit is very far away.'

But the pilgrim shrieked,

'I fear! I fear unspeakably! – and the power has departed from me!'

'The power will return, my son,' made answer the Bodhisattva . . . 'Look now below you and above you and about you, and tell me what you see.'

'I cannot,' cried the pilgrim, trembling and clinging; 'I dare not look beneath! Before me and about me there is nothing but skulls of men.'

'And yet, my son,' said the Bodhisattva, laughing softly – 'and yet you do not know of what this mountain is made.'

The other, shuddering, repeated:

'I fear! – unutterably I fear! . . . there is nothing but skulls of men!'

'A mountain of skulls it is,' responded the Bodhisattva. 'But know, my son, that all of them ARE YOUR OWN! Each has at some time been the nest of your dreams and delusions and desires. Not even one of them is the skull of any other being. All – all without exception – have been yours, in the billions of your former lives.'

A Passional Karma

One of the never-failing attractions of the Tōkyō stage is the performance, by the famous Kikugorō and his company, of the *Botan-Dōrō*, or 'Peony-Lantern'. This weird play, of which the scenes are laid in the middle of the last century, is the dramatization of a romance by the novelist Enchō, written in colloquial Japanese, and purely Japanese in local color, though inspired by a Chinese tale. I went to see the play; and Kikugorō made me familiar with a new variety of the pleasure of fear.

'Why not give English readers the ghostly part of the story?' – asked a friend who guides me betimes through the mazes of Eastern philosophy. 'It would serve to explain some popular ideas of the supernatural which Western people know very little about. And I could help you with the translation.'

I gladly accepted the suggestion; and we composed the following summary of the more extraordinary portion of Enchō's romance. Here and there we found it necessary to condense the original narrative; and we tried to keep close to the text only in the conversational passages – some of which happen to possess a particular quality of psychological interest.

This is the story of the Ghosts in the Romance of the Peony-Lantern:

I

There once lived in the district of Ushigomé, in Yedo, a *hatamoto** called Iijima Heizayémon, whose only daughter, Tsuyu, was beautiful as her name, which signifies 'Morning Dew'. Iijima took a second wife when his daughter was about sixteen; and, finding that O-Tsuyu could not be happy with her mother-in-law [*sic*], he had a pretty villa built for the girl at Yanagijima, as a separate residence, and gave her an excellent maidservant, called O-Yoné, to wait upon her.

O-Tsuyu lived happily enough in her new home until one day when the family physician, Yamamoto Shijō, paid her a visit in company with a young samurai named Hagiwara Shinzaburō, who resided in the Nedzu quarter.

---

* The *hatamoto* were samurai forming the special military force of the Shōgun. The name literally signifies 'Banner-Supporters'. These were the highest class of samurai – not only as the immediate vassals of the Shōgun, but as a military aristocracy.

Shinzaburō was an unusually handsome lad, and very gentle; and the two young people fell in love with each other at sight. Even before the brief visit was over, they contrived – unheard by the old doctor – to pledge themselves to each other for life. And, at parting, O-Tsuyu whispered to the youth, '*Remember! if you do not come to see me again, I shall certainly die!*'

Shinzaburō never forgot those words; and he was only too eager to see more of O-Tsuyu. But etiquette forbade him to make the visit alone: he was obliged to wait for some other chance to accompany the doctor, who had promised to take him to the villa a second time. Unfortunately the old man did not keep this promise. He had perceived the sudden affection of O-Tsuyu; and he feared that her father would hold him responsible for any serious results. Iijima Heizayémon had a reputation for cutting off heads. And the more Shijō thought about the possible consequences of his introduction of Shinzaburō at the Iijima villa, the more he became afraid. Therefore he purposely abstained from calling upon his young friend.

Months passed; and O-Tsuyu, little imagining the true cause of Shinzaburō's neglect, believed that her love had been scorned. Then she pined away, and died. Soon afterwards, the faithful servant O-Yoné also died, through grief at the loss of her mistress; and the two were buried side by side in the cemetery of Shin-Banzui-In – a temple which still stands in the neighborhood of Dango-Zaka, where the famous chrysanthemum-shows are yearly held.

II

Shinzaburō knew nothing of what had happened; but his disappointment and his anxiety had resulted in a prolonged illness. He was slowly recovering, but still very weak, when he unexpectedly received another visit from Yamamoto Shijō. The old man made a number of plausible excuses for his apparent neglect. Shinzaburō said to him:

'I have been sick ever since the beginning of spring; even now I cannot eat anything ... Was it not rather unkind of you never to call? I thought that we were to make another visit together to the house of the Lady Iijima; and I wanted to take to her some little present as a return for our kind reception. Of course I could not go by myself.'

Shijō gravely responded, 'I am very sorry to tell you that the young lady is dead.'

'Dead!' repeated Shinzaburō, turning white – 'did you say that she is dead?'

The doctor remained silent for a moment, as if collecting himself: then he resumed, in the quick light tone of a man resolved not to take trouble seriously:

'My great mistake was in having introduced you to

her; for it seems that she fell in love with you at once. I am afraid that you must have said something to encourage this affection – when you were in that little room together. At all events, I saw how she felt towards you; and then I became uneasy – fearing that her father might come to hear of the matter, and lay the whole blame upon me. So – to be quite frank with you – I decided that it would be better not to call upon you; and I purposely stayed away for a long time. But, only a few days ago, happening to visit Iijima's house, I heard, to my great surprise, that his daughter had died, and that her servant O-Yoné had also died. Then, remembering all that had taken place, I knew that the young lady must have died of love for you . . . [*Laughing*] Ah, you are really a sinful fellow! Yes, you are! [*Laughing*] Isn't it a sin to have been born so handsome that the girls die for love of you?* . . . [*Seriously*] Well, we must leave the dead to the dead. It is no use to talk further about the matter; all that you now can do for her is to repeat the *Nembutsu.*† . . . Good-bye.'

And the old man retired hastily – anxious to avoid further converse about the painful event for which he felt himself to have been unwittingly responsible.

---

* Perhaps this conversation may seem strange to the Western reader; but it is true to life. The whole of the scene is characteristically Japanese.
† The invocation *Namu Amida Butsu!* ('Hail to the Buddha Amitâbha!'), repeated, as a prayer, for the sake of the dead.

III

Shinzaburō long remained stupefied with grief by the news of O-Tsuyu's death. But as soon as he found himself again able to think clearly, he inscribed the dead girl's name upon a mortuary tablet, and placed the tablet in the Buddhist shrine of his house, and set offerings before it, and recited prayers. Every day thereafter he presented offerings, and repeated the *Nembutsu*; and the memory of O-Tsuyu was never absent from his thought.

Nothing occurred to change the monotony of his solitude before the time of the Bon – the great Festival of the Dead – which begins upon the thirteenth day of the seventh month. Then he decorated his house, and prepared everything for the festival; hanging out the lanterns that guide the returning spirits, and setting the food of ghosts on the *shōryōdana*, or Shelf of Souls. And on the first evening of the Bon, after sundown, he kindled a small lamp before the tablet of O-Tsuyu, and lighted the lanterns.

The night was clear, with a great moon – and windless, and very warm. Shinzaburō sought the coolness of his veranda. Clad only in a light summer-robe, he sat there thinking, dreaming, sorrowing; sometimes fanning himself; sometimes making a little smoke to drive the mosquitoes away. Everything was quiet. It was a lonesome neighborhood, and there were few passers-by. He could hear only the soft rushing of a neighboring stream, and the shrilling of night-insects.

But all at once this stillness was broken by a sound of women's *geta** approaching – *kara-kon, kara-kon*; and the sound drew nearer and nearer, quickly, till it reached the live hedge surrounding the garden. Then Shinzaburō, feeling curious, stood on tiptoe, so as to look over the hedge; and he saw two women passing. One, who was carrying a beautiful lantern decorated with peony-flowers,† appeared to be a servant; the other was a slender girl of about seventeen, wearing a long-sleeved robe embroidered with designs of autumn-blossoms. Almost at the same instant both women turned their faces toward Shinzaburō; and to his utter astonishment, he recognized O-Tsuyu and her servant O-Yoné.

They stopped immediately; and the girl cried out – 'Oh, how strange! . . . Hagiwara Sama!'

Shinzaburō simultaneously called to the maid:

---

* *Komageta* in the original. The *geta* is a wooden sandal, or clog, of which there are many varieties – some decidedly elegant. The *komageta*, or 'pony-geta' is so-called because of the sonorous hoof-like echo which it makes on hard ground.

† The sort of lantern here referred to is no longer made [. . .]. It was totally unlike the modern domestic hand-lantern, painted with the owner's crest; but it was not altogether unlike some forms of lanterns still manufactured for the Festival of the Dead, and called *Bon-dōrō*. The flowers ornamenting it were not painted: they were artificial flowers of crêpe-silk, and were attached to the top of the lantern.

'O-Yoné! Ah, you are O-Yoné! – I remember you very well.'

'Hagiwara Sama!' exclaimed O-Yoné in a tone of supreme amazement. 'Never could I have believed it possible! . . . Sir, we were told that you had died.'

'How extraordinary!' cried Shinzaburō. 'Why, I was told that both of you were dead!'

'Ah, what a hateful story!' returned O-Yoné. 'Why repeat such unlucky words? . . . Who told you?'

'Please to come in,' said Shinzaburō; 'here we can talk better. The garden-gate is open.'

So they entered, and exchanged greeting; and when Shinzaburō had made them comfortable, he said:

'I trust that you will pardon my discourtesy in not having called upon you for so long a time. But Shijō, the doctor, about a month ago, told me that you had both died.'

'So it was he who told you?' exclaimed O-Yoné. 'It was very wicked of him to say such a thing. Well, it was also Shijō who told us that you were dead. I think that he wanted to deceive you – which was not a difficult thing to do, because you are so confiding and trustful. Possibly my mistress betrayed her liking for you in some words which found their way to her father's ears; and, in that case, O-Kuni – the new wife – might have planned to make the doctor tell you that we were dead, so as to bring about a separation. Anyhow, when my mistress heard that you had died, she wanted to cut off her hair immediately, and to become a nun. But I was able to prevent her from cutting off her hair; and I

43

persuaded her at last to become a nun only in her heart. Afterwards her father wished her to marry a certain young man; and she refused. Then there was a great deal of trouble – chiefly caused by O-Kuni; and we went away from the villa, and found a very small house in Yanaka-no-Sasaki. There we are now just barely able to live, by doing a little private work . . . My mistress has been constantly repeating the *Nembutsu* for your sake. Today, being the first day of the Bon, we went to visit the temples; and we were on our way home – thus late – when this strange meeting happened.'

'Oh, how extraordinary!' cried Shinzaburō. 'Can it be true? – or is it only a dream? Here I, too, have been constantly reciting the *Nembutsu* before a tablet with her name upon it! Look!' And he showed them O-Tsuyu's tablet in its place upon the Shelf of Souls.

'We are more than grateful for your kind remembrance,' returned O-Yoné, smiling . . . 'Now as for my mistress' – she continued, turning towards O-Tsuyu, who had all the while remained demure and silent, half-hiding her face with her sleeve – 'as for my mistress, she actually says that she would not mind being disowned by her father for the time of seven existences,* or even being

---

* 'For the time of seven existences' – that is to say, for the time of seven successive lives. In Japanese drama and romance it is not uncommon to represent a father as disowning his child 'for the time of seven lives'. Such a disowning is called *shichi-shō madé no mandō*, a disinheritance for seven lives – signifying that in six future lives after the present the erring son or daughter will continue to feel the parental displeasure.

killed by him, for your sake! . . . Come! will you not allow her to stay here to-night?'

Shinzaburō turned pale for joy. He answered in a voice trembling with emotion:

'Please remain; but do not speak loud – because there is a troublesome fellow living close by – a *ninsomi** called Hakuōdō Yusai, who tells people's fortunes by looking at their faces. He is inclined to be curious; and it is better that he should not know.'

The two women remained that night in the house of the young samurai, and returned to their own home a little before daybreak. And after that night they came every night for seven nights – whether the weather were foul or fair – always at the same hour. And Shinzaburō became more and more attached to the girl; and the twain were fettered, each to each, by that bond of illusion which is stronger than bands of iron.

IV

Now there was a man called Tomozō, who lived in a small cottage adjoining Shinzaburō's residence. Tomozō and his wife O-Miné were both employed by Shinzaburō as servants. Both seemed to be devoted to their young

---

* The profession is not yet extinct. The *ninsomi* uses a kind of magnifying glass (or magnifying-mirror sometimes), called *tengankyō* or *ninsomégané*.

master; and by his help they were able to live in comparative comfort.

One night, at a very late hour, Tomozō heard the voice of a woman in his master's apartment; and this made him uneasy. He feared that Shinzaburō, being very gentle and affectionate, might be made the dupe of some cunning wanton – in which event the domestics would be the first to suffer. He therefore resolved to watch; and on the following night he stole on tiptoe to Shinzaburō's dwelling, and looked through a chink in one of the sliding-shutters. By the glow of a night-lantern within the sleeping-room, he was able to perceive that his master and a strange woman were talking together under the mosquito-net. At first he could not see the woman distinctly. Her back was turned to him; he only observed that she was very slim, and that she appeared to be very young – judging from the fashion of her dress and hair.* Putting his ear to the chink, he could hear the conversation plainly. The woman said:

'And if I should be disowned by my father, would you then let me come and live with you?'

Shinzaburō answered:

'Most assuredly I would – nay, I should be glad of the chance. But there is no reason to fear that you will ever be disowned by your father; for you are his only daughter,

---

* The color and form of the dress, and the style of wearing the hair, are by Japanese custom regulated according to the age of the woman.

and he loves you very much. What I do fear is that some day we shall be cruelly separated.'

She responded softly:

'Never, never could I even think of accepting any other man for my husband. Even if our secret were to become known, and my father were to kill me for what I have done, still – after death itself – I could never cease to think of you. And I am now quite sure that you yourself would not be able to live very long without me.' . . . Then clinging closely to him, with her lips at his neck, she caressed him; and he returned her caresses.

Tomozō wondered as he listened – because the language of the woman was not the language of a common woman, but the language of a lady of rank.* Then he determined at all hazards to get one glimpse of her face; and he crept round the house, backwards and forwards, peering through every crack and chink. And at last he was able to see; but therewith an icy trembling seized him; and the hair of his head stood up.

For the face was the face of a woman long dead – and the fingers caressing were fingers of naked bone – and of the body below the waist there was not anything: it melted off into thinnest trailing shadow. Where the eyes

---

* The forms of speech used by the samurai, and other superior classes, differed considerably from those of the popular idiom; but these differences could not be effectively rendered into English.

of the lover deluded saw youth and grace and beauty, there appeared to the eyes of the watcher horror only, and the emptiness of death. Simultaneously another woman's figure, and a weirder, rose up from within the chamber, and swiftly made toward the watcher, as if discerning his presence. Then, in uttermost terror, he fled to the dwelling of Hakuōdō Yusai, and, knocking frantically at the doors, succeeded in arousing him.

V

Hakuōdō Yusai, the *ninsomi*, was a very old man; but in his time he had travelled much, and he had heard and seen so many things that he could not be easily surprised. Yet the story of the terrified Tomozō both alarmed and amazed him. He had read in ancient Chinese books of love between the living and the dead; but he had never believed it possible. Now, however, he felt convinced that the statement of Tomozō was not a falsehood, and that something very strange was really going on in the house of Hagiwara. Should the truth prove to be what Tomozō imagined, then the young samurai was a doomed man.

'If the woman be a ghost,' said Yusai to the frightened servant, '– if the woman be a ghost, your master must die very soon – unless something extraordinary can be done to save him. And if the woman be a ghost, the signs of death will appear upon his face. For the spirit of the living is *yōki*, and pure – the spirit of the dead is *inki*, and unclean: the one is Positive, the other Negative. He whose bride is a ghost cannot live. Even though in his blood there existed the force of a life of one hundred years, that force must quickly perish . . . Still, I shall do all that I can to save Hagiwara Sama. And in the meantime, Tomozō, say nothing to any other person – not even to your wife – about this matter. At sunrise I shall call upon your master.'

VI

When questioned next morning by Yusai, Shinzaburō at first attempted to deny that any women had been visiting the house; but finding this artless policy of no avail, and perceiving that the old man's purpose was altogether unselfish, he was finally persuaded to acknowledge what had really occurred, and to give his reasons for wishing to keep the matter a secret. As for the lady Iijima, he intended, he said, to make her his wife as soon as possible.

'Oh, madness!' cried Yusai – losing all patience in the intensity of his alarm. 'Know, sir, that the people who have been coming here, night after night, are dead! Some frightful delusion is upon you! . . . Why, the simple fact that you long supposed O-Tsuyu to be dead, and repeated the *Nembutsu* for her, and made offerings before her tablet, is itself the proof! . . . The lips of the dead have touched you! – the hands of the dead have caressed you! . . . Even at this moment I see in your face the signs of death – and you will not believe! . . . Listen to me now, sir – I beg of you – if you wish to save yourself: otherwise you have less than twenty days to live. They told you – those people – that they were residing in the district of Shitaya, in Yanaka-no-Sasaki. Did you ever visit them at that place? No! – of course you did not! Then go to-day – as soon as you can – to Yanaka-no-Sasaki, and try to find their home! . . .'

And having uttered this counsel with the most vehement earnestness, Hakuōdō Yusai abruptly took his departure.

Shinzaburō, startled though not convinced, resolved after a moment's reflection to follow the advice of the *ninsomi*, and to go to Shitaya. It was yet early in the morning when he reached the quarter of Yanaka-no-Sasaki, and began his search for the dwelling of O-Tsuyu. He went through every street and side-street, read all the names inscribed at the various entrances, and made inquiries whenever an opportunity presented itself. But he could not find anything resembling the little house mentioned by O-Yoné; and none of the people whom he questioned knew of any house in the quarter inhabited by two single women. Feeling at last certain that further research would be useless, he turned homeward by the shortest way, which happened to lead through the grounds of the temple Shin-Banzui-In.

Suddenly his attention was attracted by two new tombs, placed side by side, at the rear of the temple. One was a common tomb, such as might have been erected for a person of humble rank: the other was a large and handsome monument; and hanging before it was a beautiful peony-lantern, which had probably been left there at the time of the Festival of the Dead. Shinzaburō remembered that the peony-lantern carried by O-Yoné was exactly similar; and the coincidence impressed him as strange. He looked again at the tombs; but the tombs explained nothing. Neither bore any personal name – only the Buddhist *kaimyō* or posthumous appellation. Then he determined to seek information at the temple. An acolyte stated, in reply to his questions, that the large tomb had been recently erected for the daughter of Iijima Heizayémon, the *hatamoto* of Ushigomé; and that the small tomb next to it was that of her servant O-Yoné, who had died of grief soon after the young lady's funeral.

Immediately to Shinzaburō's memory there recurred, with another and sinister meaning, the words of O-Yoné: '*We went away, and found a very small house in Yanaka-no-Sasaki. There we are now just barely able to live – by doing a little private work . . .*' Here was indeed the very small house – and in Yanaka-no-Sasaki. But the little *private work . . .* ?

Terror-stricken, the samurai hastened with all speed to the house of Yusai, and begged for his counsel and assistance. But Yusai declared himself unable to be of any aid in such a case. All that he could do was to send Shinzaburō to the high-priest Ryōseki, of Shin-Banzui-In, with a letter praying for immediate religious help.

VII

The high-priest Ryōseki was a learned and a holy man. By spiritual vision he was able to know the secret of any sorrow, and the nature of the karma that had caused it. He heard unmoved the story of Shinzaburō, and said to him:

'A very great danger now threatens you, because of an error committed in one of your former states of existence. The karma that binds you to the dead is very strong; but if I tried to explain its character, you would not be able to understand. I shall therefore tell you only this – that the dead person has no desire to injure you out of hate, feels no enmity towards you: she is influenced, on the contrary, by the most passionate affection for you. Probably the girl has been in love with you from a time long preceding your present life – from a time of not less than three or four past existences; and it would seem that, although necessarily changing her form and condition at each succeeding birth, she has not been able to cease from

following after you. Therefore it will not be an easy thing
to escape from her influence . . . But now I am going to
lend you this powerful *mamori*.* It is a pure gold image
of that Buddha called the Sea-Sounding Tathâgata – *Kai-
On-Nyōrai* – because his preaching of the Law sounds
through the world like the sound of the sea. And this little
image is especially a *shiryō-yoké*† – which protects the living from the dead. This you must wear, in its covering,
next to your body – under the girdle . . . Besides, I shall
presently perform in the temple, a *ségaki*-service‡ for the
repose of the troubled spirit . . . And here is a holy sutra,

---

* The Japanese word *mamori* has significations at least as numerous as
those attaching to our own term 'amulet'. It would be impossible, in a
mere footnote, even to suggest the variety of Japanese religious objects
to which the name is given. In this instance, the *mamori* is a very small
image, probably enclosed in a miniature shrine of lacquer-work or metal,
over which a silk cover is drawn. Such little images were often worn by
samurai on the person. I was recently shown a miniature figure of Kwannon, in an iron case, which had been carried by an officer through the
Satsuma war. He observed, with good reason, that it had probably saved
his life; for it had stopped a bullet of which the dent was plainly
visible.

† From *shiryō*, a ghost, and *yokeru*, to exclude. The Japanese have two
kinds of ghosts proper in their folklore: the spirits of the dead, *shiryō*;
and the spirits of the living, *ikiryō*. A house or a person may be haunted
by an *ikiryō* as well as by a *shiryō*.

‡ A special service – accompanying offerings of food, etc., to those dead
having no living relatives or friends to care for them – is thus termed.
In this case, however, the service would be of a particular and exceptional
kind.

called *Ubō-Darani-Kyō*, or "Treasure-Raining Sutra":* you must be careful to recite it every night in your house without fail . . . Furthermore I shall give you this package of *o-fuda*;† you must paste one of them over every opening of your house – no matter how small. If you do this, the power of the holy texts will prevent the dead from entering. But – whatever may happen – do not fail to recite the sutra.'

Shinzaburō humbly thanked the high-priest and then, taking with him the image, the sutra, and the bundle of sacred texts, he made all haste to reach his home before the hour of sunset.

* The name would be more correctly written *Uhō-Darani-Kyō*. It is the Japanese pronunciation of the title of a very short sutra translated out of Sanscrit into Chinese by the Indian priest Amoghavajra, probably during the eighth century. The Chinese text contains transliterations of some mysterious Sanscrit words – apparently talismanic words – like those to be seen in Kern's translation of the Saddharma-Pundarika, ch. xxvi.

† *O-fuda* is the general name given to religious texts used as charms or talismans. They are sometimes stamped or burned upon wood, but more commonly written or printed upon narrow strips of paper. *O-fuda* are pasted above house-entrances, on the walls of rooms, upon tablets placed in household shrines, etc., etc. Some kinds are worn about the person; others are made into pellets, and swallowed as spiritual medicine. The text of the larger *o-fuda* is often accompanied by curious pictures or symbolic illustrations.

VIII

With Yusai's advice and help, Shinzaburō was able before dark to fix the holy texts over all the apertures of his dwelling. Then the *ninsomi* returned to his own house – leaving the youth alone.

Night came, warm and clear. Shinzaburō made fast the doors, bound the precious amulet about his waist, entered his mosquito-net, and by the glow of a night-lantern began to recite the *Ubō-Darani-Kyō*. For a long time he chanted the words, comprehending little of their meaning; then he tried to obtain some rest. But his mind was still too much disturbed by the strange events of the day. Midnight passed; and no sleep came to him. At last he heard the boom of the great temple-bell of Dentsu-In announcing the eighth hour.*

It ceased; and Shinzaburō suddenly heard the sound of *geta* approaching from the old direction – but this time more slowly: *karan-koron, karan-koron!* At once a cold

---

* According to the old Japanese way of counting time, this *yatsudoki* or eighth hour was the same as our two o'clock in the morning. Each Japanese hour was equal to two European hours, so that there were only six hours instead of our twelve; and these six hours were counted backwards in the order, 9, 8, 7, 6, 5, 4. Thus the ninth hour corresponded to our midday, or midnight; half-past nine to our one o'clock; eight to our two o'clock. Two o'clock in the morning, also called 'the Hour of the Ox', was the Japanese hour of ghosts and goblins.

sweat broke over his forehead. Opening the sutra hastily, with trembling hand, he began again to recite it aloud. The steps came nearer and nearer – reached the live hedge – stopped! Then, strange to say, Shinzaburō felt unable to remain under his mosquito-net: something stronger even than his fear impelled him to look; and, instead of continuing to recite the *Ubō-Darani-Kyō*, he foolishly approached the shutters, and through a chink peered out into the night. Before the house be saw O-Tsuyu standing, and O-Yoné with the peony-lantern; and both of them were gazing at the Buddhist texts pasted above the entrance. Never before – not even in what time she lived – had O-Tsuyu appeared so beautiful; and Shinzaburō felt his heart drawn towards her with a power almost resistless. But the terror of death and the terror of the unknown restrained; and there went on within him such a struggle between his love and his fear that he became as one suffering in the body the pains of the Shō-netsu hell.* Presently he heard the voice of the maid-servant, saying: 'My dear mistress, there is no way to enter. The heart of Hagiwara Sama must have changed. For the promise that he made last night has been broken; and the doors have been made fast to keep us out . . . We

* *En-netsu* or *Shō-netsu* (Sanscrit 'Tapana') is the sixth of the Eight Hot Hells of Japanese Buddhism. One day of life in this hell is equal in duration to thousands (some say millions) of human years.

cannot go in to-night . . . It will be wiser for you to make up your mind not to think any more about him, because his feeling towards you has certainly changed. It is evident that he does not want to see you. So it will be better not to give yourself any more trouble for the sake of a man whose heart is so unkind.'

But the girl answered, weeping:

'Oh, to think that this could happen after the pledges which we made to each other! . . . Often I was told that the heart of a man changes as quickly as the sky of autumn; yet surely the heart of Hagiwara Sama cannot be so cruel that he should really intend to exclude me in this way! . . . Dear Yoné, please find some means of taking me to him . . . Unless you do, I will never, never go home again.'

Thus she continued to plead, veiling her face with her long sleeves – and very beautiful she looked, and very touching; but the fear of death was strong upon her lover.

O-Yoné at last made answer,

'My dear young lady, why will you trouble your mind about a man who seems to be so cruel? . . . Well, let us see if there be no way to enter at the back of the house: come with me!'

And taking O-Tsuyu by the hand, she led her away toward the rear of the dwelling; and there the two disappeared as suddenly as the light disappears when the flame of a lamp is blown out.

IX

Night after night the shadows came at the Hour of the Ox; and nightly Shinzaburō heard the weeping of O-Tsuyu. Yet he believed himself saved – little imagining that his doom had already been decided by the character of his dependants.

Tomozō had promised Yusai never to speak to any other person – not even to O-Miné – of the strange events that were taking place. But Tomozō was not long suffered by the haunters to rest in peace. Night after night O-Yoné entered into his dwelling, and roused him from his sleep, and asked him to remove the *o-fuda* placed over one very small window at the back of his master's house. And Tomozō, out of fear, as often promised her to take away the *o-fuda* before the next sundown; but never by day could he make up his mind to remove it – believing that evil was intended to Shinzaburō. At last, in a night of storm, O-Yoné startled him from slumber with a cry of reproach, and stooped above his pillow, and said to him: 'Have a care how you trifle with us! If, by to-morrow night, you do not take away that text, you shall learn how I can hate!' And she made her face so frightful as she spoke that Tomozō nearly died of terror.

O-Miné, the wife of Tomozō, had never till then known of these visits: even to her husband they had seemed like bad dreams. But on this particular night it chanced that, waking suddenly, she heard the voice of a woman talking to Tomozō. Almost in the same moment the talking ceased; and when O-Miné looked about her, she saw, by the light of the night-lamp, only her husband, shuddering and white with fear. The stranger was gone; the doors were fast: it seemed impossible that anybody could have entered. Nevertheless the jealousy of the wife had been aroused; and she began to chide and to question Tomozō in such a manner that he thought himself obliged to betray the secret, and to explain the terrible dilemma in which he had been placed.

Then the passion of O-Miné yielded to wonder and alarm; but she was a subtle woman, and she devised immediately a plan to save her husband by the sacrifice of her master. And she gave Tomozō a cunning counsel – telling him to make conditions with the dead.

They came again on the following night at the Hour of the Ox; and O-Miné hid herself on hearing the sound of their coming – *karan-koron, karan-koron!* But Tomozō went out to meet them in the dark, and even found courage to say to them what his wife had told him to say:

'It is true that I deserve your blame; but I had no wish to cause you anger. The reason that the *o-fuda* has not been taken away is that my wife and I are able to live only by the help of Hagiwara Sama, and that we cannot expose him to any danger without bringing misfortune upon ourselves. But if we could obtain the sum of a hundred *ryō* in gold, we should be able to please you, because we should then need no help from anybody. Therefore if you will give us a hundred *ryō*, I can take the *o-fuda* away without being afraid of losing our only means of support.'

When he had uttered these words, O-Yoné and O-Tsuyu looked at each other in silence for a moment. Then O-Yoné said:

'Mistress, I told you that it was not right to trouble this man – as we have no just cause of ill will against him. But it is certainly useless to fret yourself about Hagiwara Sama, because his heart has changed towards you. Now once again, my dear young lady, let me beg you not to think any more about him!'

But O-Tsuyu, weeping, made answer:

'Dear Yoné, whatever may happen, I cannot possibly keep myself from thinking about him! . . . You know that you can get a hundred *ryō* to have the *o-fuda* taken off . . . Only once more, I pray, dear Yoné! – only once more bring me face to face with Hagiwara Sama – I beseech you!' And hiding her face with her sleeve, she thus continued to plead.

'Oh! why will you ask me to do these things?' responded O-Yoné. 'You know very well that I have no money. But since you will persist in this whim of yours, in spite of all that I can say, I suppose that I must try to find the money somehow, and to bring it here to-morrow night . . .' Then, turning to the faithless Tomozō,

she said: 'Tomozō, I must tell you that Hagiwara Sama
now wears upon his body a *mamori* called by the name
of *Kai-On-Nyōrai*, and that so long as he wears it we cannot approach him. So you will have to get that *mamori*
away from him, by some means or other, as well as to
remove the *o-fuda*.'

Tomozō feebly made answer:

'That also I can do, if you will promise to bring me the
hundred *ryō*.'

'Well, mistress,' said O-Yoné, 'you will wait – will you
not – until to-morrow night?'

'Oh, dear Yoné!' sobbed the other – 'have we to go
back to-night again without seeing Hagiwara Sama? Ah!
it is cruel!'

And the shadow of the mistress, weeping, was led away
by the shadow of the maid.

X

Another day went, and another night came, and the dead
came with it. But this time no lamentation was heard
without the house of Hagiwara; for the faithless servant
found his reward at the Hour of the Ox, and removed the
o-fuda. Moreover he had been able, while his master was
at the bath, to steal from its case the golden *mamori*,
and to substitute for it an image of copper; and he had buried
the *Kai-On-Nyōrai* in a desolate field. So the visitants

found nothing to oppose their entering. Veiling their faces with their sleeves they rose and passed, like a streaming of vapor, into the little window from over which the holy text had been torn away. But what happened thereafter within the house Tomozō never knew.

The sun was high before he ventured again to approach his master's dwelling, and to knock upon the sliding-doors. For the first time in years he obtained no response; and the silence made him afraid. Repeatedly he called, and received no answer. Then, aided by O-Miné, he succeeded in effecting an entrance and making his way alone to the sleeping-room, where he called again in vain. He rolled back the rumbling shutters to admit the light; but still within the house there was no stir. At last he dared to lift a corner of the mosquito-net. But no sooner had he looked beneath than he fled from the house, with a cry of horror.

Shinzaburō was dead – hideously dead; and his face was the face of a man who had died in the uttermost agony of fear; and lying beside him in the bed were the bones of a woman! And the bones of the arms, and the bones of the hands, clung fast about his neck.

XI

Hakuōdō Yusai, the fortune-teller, went to view the corpse at the prayer of the faithless Tomozō. The old man was terrified and astonished at the spectacle, but looked about him with a keen eye. He soon perceived that the *o-fuda* had been taken from the little window at the back of the house; and on searching the body of Shinzaburō, he discovered that the golden *mamori* had been taken from its wrapping, and a copper image of Fudō put in place of it. He suspected Tomozō of the theft; but the whole occurrence was so very extraordinary that he thought it prudent to consult with the priest Ryōseki before taking further action. Therefore, after having made a careful examination of the premises, he betook himself to the temple Shin-Banzui-In, as quickly as his aged limbs could bear him.

Ryōseki, without waiting to hear the purpose of the old man's visit, at once invited him into a private apartment.

'You know that you are always welcome here,' said Ryōseki. 'Please seat yourself at ease . . . Well, I am sorry to tell you that Hagiwara Sama is dead.'

Yusai wonderingly exclaimed:

'Yes, he is dead; but how did you learn of it?'

The priest responded:

'Hagiwara Sama was suffering from the results of an evil karma; and his attendant was a bad man. What happened to Hagiwara Sama was unavoidable; his destiny had been determined from a time long before his last birth. It will be better for you not to let your mind be troubled by this event.'

Yusai said:

'I have heard that a priest of pure life may gain power to see into the future for a hundred years; but truly this is the first time in my existence that I have had proof of such power . . . Still, there is another matter about which I am very anxious . . .'

'You mean,' interrupted Ryōseki, 'the stealing of the holy *mamori*, the *Kai-On-Nyōrai*. But you must not give yourself any concern about that. The image has been buried in a field; and it will be found there and returned to me during the eighth month of the coming year. So please do not be anxious about it.'

More and more amazed, the old *ninsomi* ventured to observe:

'I have studied the *In-Yō*,* and the science of divination; and I make my living by telling people's fortunes; but I cannot possibly understand how you know these things.'

Ryōseki answered gravely:

'Never mind how I happen to know them . . . I now want to speak to you about Hagiwara's funeral. The House of Hagiwara has its own family-cemetery, of course; but to bury him there would not be proper. He must be buried beside O-Tsuyu, the Lady Iijima; for his karma-relation to her was a very deep one. And it is but

---

* The Male and Female principles of the universe, the Active and Passive forces of Nature. Yusai refers here to the old Chinese nature-philosophy – better known to Western readers by the name FENG-SHUI.

right that you should erect a tomb for him at your own cost, because you have been indebted to him for many favors.'

Thus it came to pass that Shinzaburō was buried beside O-Tsuyu, in the cemetery of Shin-Banzui-In, in Yanaka-no-Sasaki.

Here ends the story of the Ghosts in the Romance of the Peony-Lantern.

My friend asked me whether the story had interested me; and I answered by telling him that I wanted to go to the cemetery of Shin-Banzui-In, so as to realize more definitely the local color of the author's studies.

'I shall go with you at once,' he said. 'But what did you think of the personages?'

'To Western thinking,' I made answer, 'Shinzaburō is a despicable creature. I have been mentally comparing him with the true lovers of our old ballad-literature. They were only too glad to follow a dead sweetheart into the grave; and nevertheless, being Christians, they believed that they had only one human life to enjoy in this world. But Shinzaburō was a Buddhist – with a million lives behind him and a million lives before him; and he was too selfish to give up even one miserable existence for the sake of the girl that came back to him from the dead. Then he was even more cowardly than selfish. Although a samurai by birth and training, he had to beg a priest to save him from ghosts. In every way he proved himself contemptible; and O-Tsuyu did quite right in choking him to death.'

'From the Japanese point of view, likewise,' my friend responded, 'Shinzaburō is rather contemptible. But the use of this weak character helped the author to develop incidents that could not otherwise, perhaps, have been so effectively managed. To my thinking, the only attractive character in the story is that of O-Yoné: type of the old-time loyal and loving servant – intelligent, shrewd, full of resource – faithful not only unto death, but beyond death . . . Well, let us go to Shin-Banzui-In.'

We found the temple uninteresting, and the cemetery an abomination of desolation. Spaces once occupied by graves had been turned into potato-patches. Between were tombs leaning at all angles out of the perpendicular, tablets made illegible by scurf, empty pedestals, shattered water-tanks, and statues of Buddhas without heads or hands. Recent rains had soaked the black soil, leaving here and there small pools of slime about which swarms of tiny frogs were hopping. Everything – excepting the potato-patches – seemed to have been neglected for years. In a shed just within the gate, we observed a woman cooking; and my companion presumed to ask her if she knew anything about the tombs described in the Romance of the Peony-Lantern.

'Ah! the tombs of O-Tsuyu and O-Yoné?' she responded, smiling; 'you will find them near the end of the first row at the back of the temple – next to the statue of Jizō.'

Surprises of this kind I had met with elsewhere in Japan.

We picked our way between the rain-pools and between the green ridges of young potatoes – whose roots were doubtless feeding on the substance of many another O-Tsuyu and O-Yoné; and we reached at last two lichen-eaten tombs of which the inscriptions seemed almost obliterated. Beside the larger tomb was a statue of Jizō, with a broken nose.

'The characters are not easy to make out,' said my friend – 'but wait!' . . . He drew from his sleeve a sheet of soft white paper, laid it over the inscription, and began to rub the paper with a lump of clay. As he did so, the characters appeared in white on the blackened surface.

' "*Eleventh day, third month – Rat, Elder Brother, Fire – Sixth year of Horéki* [AD 1756]." . . . This would seem to be the grave of some innkeeper of Nedzu, named Kichibei. Let us see what is on the other monument.'

With a fresh sheet of paper he presently brought out the text of a *kaimyō*, and read,

' "*En-myō-In, Hō-yō-I-tei-ken-shi, Hō-ni*": "*Nun-of-the-Law, Illustrious, Pure-of-heart-and-will, Famed-in-the-Law – inhabiting the Mansion-of-the-Preaching-of-Wonder*" . . . The grave of some Buddhist nun.'

'What utter humbug!' I exclaimed. 'That woman was only making fun of us.'

'Now,' my friend protested, 'you are unjust to the woman! You came here because you wanted a sensation; and she tried her very best to please you. You did not suppose that ghost-story was true, did you?'

Ingwa-Banashi

The *daimyō*'s wife was dying, and knew that she was dying. She had not been able to leave her bed since the early autumn of the tenth Bunsei. It was now the fourth month of the twelfth Bunsei – the year 1829 by Western counting; and the cherry-trees were blossoming. She thought of the cherry-trees in her garden, and of the gladness of spring. She thought of her children. She thought of her husband's various concubines – especially the Lady Yukiko, nineteen years old.

'My dear wife,' said the *daimyō*, 'you have suffered very much for three long years. We have done all that we could to get you well – watching beside you night and day, praying for you, and often fasting for your sake. But in spite of our loving care, and in spite of the skill of our best physicians, it would now seem that the end of your life is not far off. Probably we shall sorrow more than you will sorrow because of your having to leave what the Buddha so truly termed "this burning-house of the world". I shall order to be performed – no matter what the cost – every religious rite that can serve you in regard to your next rebirth; and all of us will pray without ceasing for you, that you may not have to wander in the Black Space, but may quickly enter Paradise, and attain to Buddhahood.'

He spoke with the utmost tenderness, caressing her the while. Then, with eyelids closed, she answered him in a voice thin as the voice of an insect:

'I am grateful – most grateful – for your kind words . . . Yes, it is true, as you say, that I have been sick for three long years, and that I have been treated with all possible care and affection . . . Why, indeed, should I turn away from the one true Path at the very moment of my death? . . . Perhaps to think of worldly matters at such a time is not right; but I have one last request to make – only one . . . Call here to me the Lady Yukiko; you know that I love her like a sister. I want to speak to her about the affairs of this household.'

Yukiko came at the summons of the lord, and, in obedience to a sign from him, knelt down beside the couch. The *daimyō*'s wife opened her eyes, and looked at Yukiko, and spoke:

'Ah, here is Yukiko! . . . I am so pleased to see you, Yukiko! . . . Come a little closer – so that you can hear me well: I am not able to speak loud . . . Yukiko, I am going to die. I hope that you will be faithful in all things to our dear lord; for I want you to take my place when I am gone . . . I hope that you will always be loved by him – yes, even a hundred times more than I have been – and that you will very soon be promoted to a higher rank, and become his honored wife . . . And I beg of you always to cherish our dear lord: never allow another woman to rob you of his affection . . . This is what I wanted to say to you, dear Yukiko . . . Have you been able to understand?'

'Oh, my dear Lady,' protested Yukiko, 'do not, I entreat you, say such strange things to me! You well know that I am of poor and mean condition: how could I ever dare to aspire to become the wife of our lord!'

'Nay, nay!' returned the wife, huskily – 'this is not a time for words of ceremony: let us speak only the truth to each other. After my death, you will certainly be promoted to a higher place; and I now assure you again that I wish you to become the wife of our lord – yes, I wish this, Yukiko, even more than I wish to become a Buddha! . . . Ah, I had almost forgotten! – I want you to do something for me, Yukiko. You know that in the garden there is a *yaë-zakura*,* which was brought here, the year before last, from Mount Yoshino in Yamato. I have been told that it is now in full bloom; and I wanted so much to see it in flower! In a little while I shall be dead; I must see that tree before I die. Now I wish you to carry me into the garden – at once, Yukiko – so that I can see it . . . Yes, upon your back, Yukiko; take me upon your back . . .'

While thus asking, her voice had gradually become clear and strong – as if the intensity of the wish had given her

---

* *Yaë-zakura*, *yaë-no-sakura*, a variety of Japanese cherry-tree that bears double-blossoms.

new force: then she suddenly burst into tears. Yukiko knelt motionless, not knowing what to do; but the lord nodded assent.

'It is her last wish in this world,' he said. 'She always loved cherry-flowers; and I know that she wanted very much to see that Yamato-tree in blossom. Come, my dear Yukiko, let her have her will.'

As a nurse turns her back to a child, that the child may cling to it, Yukiko offered her shoulders to the wife, and said:

'Lady, I am ready: please tell me how I best can help you.'

'Why, this way!' – responded the dying woman, lifting herself with an almost superhuman effort by clinging to Yukiko's shoulders. But as she stood erect, she quickly slipped her thin hands down over the shoulders, under the robe, and clutched the breasts of the girl, and burst into a wicked laugh.

'I have my wish!' she cried – 'I have my wish for the cherry-bloom* – but not the cherry-bloom of the garden! . . . I could not die before I got my wish. Now I have it! – oh, what a delight!' And with these words she fell forward upon the crouching girl, and died.

*

* In Japanese poetry and proverbial phraseology, the physical beauty of a woman is compared to the cherry-flower; while feminine moral beauty is compared to the plum-flower.

The attendants at once attempted to lift the body from Yukiko's shoulders, and to lay it upon the bed. But – strange to say! – this seemingly easy thing could not be done. The cold hands had attached themselves in some unaccountable way to the breasts of the girl – appeared to have grown into the quick flesh. Yukiko became senseless with fear and pain.

Physicians were called. They could not understand what had taken place. By no ordinary methods could the hands of the dead woman be unfastened from the body of her victim; they so clung that any effort to remove them brought blood. This was not because the fingers held: it was because the flesh of the palms had united itself in some inexplicable manner to the flesh of the breasts!

At that time the most skilful physician in Yedo was a foreigner – a Dutch surgeon. It was decided to summon him. After a careful examination he said that he could not understand the case, and that for the immediate relief of Yukiko there was nothing to be done except to cut the hands from the corpse. He declared that it would be dangerous to attempt to detach them from the breasts. His advice was accepted; and the hands were amputated at the wrists. But they remained clinging to the breasts; and there they soon darkened and dried up – like the hands of a person long dead.

Yet this was only the beginning of the horror.

Withered and bloodless though they seemed, those hands were not dead. At intervals they would stir – stealthily, like great gray spiders. And nightly thereafter – beginning always at the Hour of the Ox* – they would clutch and compress and torture. Only at the Hour of the Tiger the pain would cease.

Yukiko cut off her hair, and became a mendicant-nun – taking the religious name of Dassetsu. She had an *ihai* (mortuary tablet) made, bearing the *kaimyō* of her dead mistress – '*Myō-Kō-In-Den Chizan-Ryō-Fu Daishi*'; and this she carried about with her in all her wanderings; and every day before it she humbly besought the dead for pardon, and performed a Buddhist service in order that the jealous spirit might find rest. But the evil karma that had rendered such an affliction possible could not soon be exhausted. Every night at the Hour of the Ox, the hands never failed to torture her, during more than seventeen years – according to the testimony of those persons to whom she last told her story, when she stopped for one evening at the house of Noguchi Dengozayémon, in the village of Tanaka in the district of Kawachi in the province of Shimotsuké. This was in the third year of Kōkwa (1846). Thereafter nothing more was ever heard of her.

---

* In ancient Japanese time, the Hour of the Ox was the special hour of ghosts. It began at 2 AM, and lasted until 4 AM – for the old Japanese hour was double the length of the modern hour. The Hour of the Tiger began at 4 AM.

The Corpse-Rider

The body was cold as ice; the heart had long ceased to beat:
yet there were no other signs of death. Nobody even spoke
of burying the woman. She had died of grief and anger at
having been divorced. It would have been useless to bury
her – because the last undying wish of a dying person for
vengeance can burst asunder any tomb and lift the heaviest
graveyard stone. People who lived near the house in which
she was lying fled from their homes. They knew that she
was only *waiting for the return of the man who had divorced her*.

At the time of her death he was on a journey. When he
came back and was told what had happened, terror seized
him. 'If I can find no help before dark,' he thought to himself, 'she will tear me to pieces.' It was yet only the Hour of
the Dragon;* but he knew that he had no time to lose.

He went at once to an *inyōshi*† and begged for succor.
The *inyōshi* knew the story of the dead woman; and he had

---

* *Tatsu no Koku*, or the Hour of the Dragon, by old Japanese time, began
at about eight o'clock in the morning.
† *Inyōshi*, a professor or master of the science of *in-yō* – the old Chinese
nature-philosophy, based upon the theory of a male and a female prin-
ciple pervading the universe.

75

seen the body. He said to the supplicant: 'A very great danger threatens you. I will try to save you. But you must promise to do whatever I shall tell you to do. There is only one way by which you can be saved. It is a fearful way. But unless you find the courage to attempt it, she will tear you limb from limb. If you can be brave, come to me again in the evening before sunset.' The man shuddered; but he promised to do whatever should be required of him.

At sunset the *inyōshi* went with him to the house where the body was lying. The *inyōshi* pushed open the sliding-doors, and told his client to enter. It was rapidly growing dark. 'I dare not!' gasped the man, quaking from head to foot; 'I dare not even look at her!' 'You will have to do much more than look at her,' declared the *inyōshi*; 'and you promised to obey. Go in!' He forced the trembler into the house and led him to the side of the corpse.

The dead woman was lying on her face. 'Now you must get astride upon her,' said the *inyōshi*, 'and sit firmly on her back, as if you were riding a horse . . . Come! – you must do it!' The man shivered so that the *inyōshi* had to support him – shivered horribly; but he obeyed. 'Now take her hair in your hands,' commanded the *inyōshi* – 'half in the right hand, half in the left . . . So! . . . You must grip it like a bridle. Twist your hands in it – both hands – tightly. That is the way! . . . Listen to me! You must stay like that till morning. You will have reason to be afraid in the night – plenty of reason. But whatever may happen, never let go of her hair. If you let go – even for one second – she will tear you into gobbets!'

The *inyōshi* then whispered some mysterious words into the ear of the body, and said to its rider: 'Now, for my own sake, I must leave you alone with her . . . Remain as you are! . . . Above all things, remember that you must not let go of her hair.' And he went away – closing the doors behind him.

Hour after hour the man sat upon the corpse in black fear; and the hush of the night deepened and deepened about him till he screamed to break it. Instantly the body sprang beneath him, as to cast him off; and the dead woman cried out loudly, 'Oh, how heavy it is! Yet I shall bring that fellow here now!'

Then tall she rose, and leaped to the doors, and flung them open, and rushed into the night – always bearing the weight of the man. But he, shutting his eyes, kept his hands twisted in her long hair – tightly, tightly – though fearing with such a fear that he could not even moan. How far she went, he never knew. He saw nothing: he heard only the sound of her naked feet in the dark – *picha-picha*, *picha-picha* – and the hiss of her breathing as she ran.

At last she turned, and ran back into the house, and lay down upon the floor exactly as at first. Under the man she panted and moaned till the cocks began to crow. Thereafter she lay still.

But the man, with chattering teeth, sat upon her until the *inyōshi* came at sunrise. 'So you did not let go of her hair!' – observed the *inyōshi*, greatly pleased. 'That is well . . . Now you can stand up.' He whispered again into the ear of the corpse, and then said to the man: 'You must have passed a fearful night; but nothing else could have saved you. Hereafter you may feel secure from her vengeance.'

The conclusion of this story I do not think to be morally satisfying. It is not recorded that the corpse-rider became insane, or that his hair turned white: we are told only that 'he worshipped the *inyōshi* with tears of gratitude.' A note appended to the recital is equally disappointing. 'It is reported,' the Japanese author says, 'that a grandchild of the man [*who rode the corpse*] still survives, and that a grandson of the *inyōshi* is at this very time living in a village called Otokunoi-mura [*probably pronounced Otonoi-mura*].'

This village-name does not appear in any Japanese directory of today. But the names of many towns and villages have been changed since the foregoing story was written.

The Gratitude of the Samébito

There was a man named Tawaraya Tōtarō, who lived in the Province of Ōmi. His house was situated on the shore of Lake Biwa, not far from the famous temple called Ishiyamadera. He had some property, and lived in comfort; but at the age of twenty-nine he was still unmarried. His greatest ambition was to marry a very beautiful woman; and he had not been able to find a girl to his liking.

One day, as he was passing over the Long Bridge of Séta* he saw a strange being crouching close to the parapet. The body of this being resembled the body of a man, but was black as ink; its face was like the face of a demon; its eyes were green as emeralds; and its beard was like the beard of a dragon. Tōtarō was at first very much startled.

---

* The Long Bridge of Séta (*Séta-no-Naga-Hashi*), famous in Japanese legend, is nearly eight hundred feet in length, and commands a beautiful view. This bridge crosses the waters of the Setagawa near the junction of the stream with Lake Biwa. Ishiyamadera, one of the most picturesque Buddhist temples in Japan, is situated within a short distance from the bridge.

But the green eyes looked at him so gently that after a moment's hesitation he ventured to question the creature. Then it answered him, saying: 'I am a *Samébito** – a Shark-Man of the sea; and until a short time ago I was in the service of the Eight Great Dragon-Kings [*Hachi-Dai-Ryū-Ō*] as a subordinate officer in the Dragon-Palace [*Ryūgū*].† But because of a small fault which I committed, I was dismissed from the Dragon-Palace, and also banished from the Sea. Since then I have been wandering about here – unable to get any food, or even a place to lie down. If you can feel any pity for me, do, I beseech you, help me to find a shelter, and let me have something to eat!'

This petition was uttered in so plaintive a tone, and in so humble a manner, that Tōtarō's heart was touched. 'Come with me,' he said. 'There is in my garden a large and deep pond where you may live as long as you wish; and I will give you plenty to eat.'

---

* Literally, 'a Shark-Person', but in this story the *Samébito* is a male. The characters for *Samébito* can also be read *Kōjin* – which is the usual reading. In dictionaries the word is loosely rendered by 'merman' or 'mermaid'; but as the above description shows, the *Samébito* or *Kōjin* of the Far East is a conception having little in common with the Western idea of a merman or mermaid.

† *Ryūgū* is also the name given to the whole of that fairy-realm beneath the sea which figures in so many Japanese legends.

The *Samébito* followed Tōtarō home, and appeared to be much pleased with the pond.

Thereafter, for nearly half a year, this strange guest dwelt in the pond, and was every day supplied by Tōtarō with such food as sea-creatures like.

[*From this point of the original narrative the Shark-Man is referred to, not as a monster, but as a sympathetic Person of the male sex.*]

Now, in the seventh month of the same year, there was a female pilgrimage (*nyonin-mōdé*) to the great Buddhist temple called Miidera, in the neighboring town of Ōtsu; and Tōtarō went to Ōtsu to attend the festival. Among the multitude of women and young girls there assembled, he observed a person of extraordinary beauty. She seemed about sixteen years old; her face was fair and pure as snow; and the loveliness of her lips assured the beholder that their every utterance would sound 'as sweet as the voice of a nightingale singing upon a plum-tree'. Tōtarō fell in love with her at sight. When she left the temple he followed her at a respectful distance, and discovered that she and her mother were staying for a few days at a certain house in the neighboring village of Séta. By questioning some of the village folk, he was able also to learn that her name was Tamana; that she was unmarried; and that her family appeared to be unwilling that she should marry a man of ordinary rank – for they demanded as a betrothal-gift a casket containing ten thousand jewels.*

Tōtarō returned home very much dismayed by this information. The more that he thought about the strange betrothal-gift demanded by the girl's parents, the more he felt that he could never expect to obtain her for his wife. Even supposing that there were as many as ten thousand jewels in the whole country, only a great prince could hope to procure them.

But not even for a single hour could Tōtarō banish from his mind the memory of that beautiful being. It haunted him so that he could neither eat nor sleep; and it seemed to become more and more vivid as the days went by. And at last he became ill – so ill that he could not lift his head from the pillow. Then he sent for a doctor.

The doctor, after having made a careful examination, uttered an exclamation of surprise. 'Almost any kind of sickness,' he said, 'can be cured by proper medical treatment, except the sickness of love. Your ailment is evidently love-sickness. There is no cure for it. In ancient

* *Tama* in the original. This word tama has a multitude of meanings; and as here used it is quite as indefinite as our own terms 'jewel', 'gem', or 'precious stone'. Indeed, it is more indefinite, for it signifies also a bead of coral, a ball of crystal, a polished stone attached to a hairpin, etc., etc. Later on, however, I venture to render it by 'ruby' – for reasons which need no explanation.

times Rōya-Ō Hakuyo died of that sickness; and you must prepare yourself to die as he died.' So saying, the doctor went away, without even giving any medicine to Tōtarō.

About this time the Shark-Man that was living in the garden-pond heard of his master's sickness, and came into the house to wait upon Tōtarō. And he tended him with the utmost affection both by day and by night. But he did not know either the cause or the serious nature of the sickness until nearly a week later, when Tōtarō, thinking himself about to die, uttered these words of farewell:

'I suppose that I have had the pleasure of caring for you thus long, because of some relation that grew up between us in a former state of existence. But now I am very sick indeed, and every day my sickness becomes worse; and my life is like the morning dew which passes away before the setting of the sun. For your sake, therefore, I am troubled in mind. Your existence has depended upon my care; and I fear that there will be no one to care for you and to feed you when I am dead ... My poor friend! Alas! our hopes and our wishes are always disappointed in this unhappy world!'

No sooner had Tōtarō spoken these words than the *Samébito* uttered a strange wild cry of pain, and began to weep bitterly. And as he wept, great tears of blood streamed from his green eyes and rolled down his black cheeks and dripped upon the floor. And, falling, they were blood; but, having fallen, they became hard and bright and beautiful – became jewels of inestimable price, rubies splendid as crimson fire. For when men of the sea weep, their tears become precious stones.

Then Tōtarō, beholding this marvel, was so amazed and overjoyed that his strength returned to him. He sprang from his bed, and began to pick up and to count the tears of the Shark-Man, crying out the while: 'My sickness is cured! I shall live! I shall live!'

Therewith, the Shark-Man, greatly astonished, ceased to weep, and asked Tōtarō to explain this wonderful cure; and Tōtarō told him about the young person seen at Miidera, and about the extraordinary marriage-gift demanded by her family. 'As I felt sure,' added Tōtarō, 'that I should never be able to get ten thousand jewels, I supposed that my suit would be hopeless. Then I became very unhappy, and at last fell sick. But now, because of your generous weeping, I have many precious stones; and I think that I shall be able to marry that girl. Only – there are not yet quite enough stones; and I beg that you will be good enough to weep a little more, so as to make up the full number required.'

But at this request the *Samébito* shook his head, and answered in a tone of surprise and of reproach:

'Do you think that I am like a harlot – able to weep whenever I wish? Oh, no! Harlots shed tears in order to deceive men; but creatures of the sea cannot weep without feeling real sorrow. I wept for you because of the true grief that I felt in my heart at the thought that you were going to die. But now I cannot weep for you, because you have told me that your sickness is cured.'

'Then what am I to do?' plaintively asked Tōtarō. 'Unless I can get ten thousand jewels, I cannot marry the girl!'

The *Samébito* remained for a little while silent, as if thinking. Then he said:

'Listen! To-day I cannot possibly weep any more. But to-morrow let us go together to the Long Bridge of Séta, taking with us some wine and some fish. We can rest for a time on the bridge; and while we are drinking the wine and eating the fish, I shall gaze in the direction of the Dragon-Palace, and try, by thinking of the happy days that I spent there, to make myself feel homesick – so that I can weep.'

Tōtarō joyfully assented.

Next morning the two, taking plenty of wine and fish with them, went to the Séta bridge, and rested there, and feasted. After having drunk a great deal of wine, the *Samébito* began to gaze in the direction of the Dragon-Kingdom, and to think about the past. And gradually, under the softening influence of the wine, the memory of happier days filled his heart with sorrow, and the pain of homesickness came upon him, so that he could weep profusely. And the great red tears that he shed fell upon the bridge in a shower of rubies; and Tōtarō gathered them as they fell, and put them into a casket, and counted them until he had counted the full number of ten thousand. Then he uttered a shout of joy.

Almost in the same moment, from far away over the lake, a delightful sound of music was heard; and there appeared in the offing, slowly rising from the waters, like some fabric of cloud, a palace of the color of the setting sun.

At once the *Samébito* sprang upon the parapet of the bridge, and looked, and laughed for joy. Then, turning to Tōtarō, he said:

'There must have been a general amnesty proclaimed in the Dragon-Realm; the Kings are calling me. So now I must bid you farewell. I am happy to have had one chance of befriending you in return for your goodness to me.'

With these words he leaped from the bridge; and no man ever saw him again. But Tōtarō presented the casket of red jewels to the parents of Tamana, and so obtained her in marriage.

Of a Promise Kept*

'I shall return in the early autumn,' said Akana Soyëmon several hundred years ago, – when bidding good-bye to his brother by adoption, young Hasébé Samon. The time was spring; and the place was the village of Kato in the province of Harima. Akana was an Izumo samurai; and he wanted to visit his birthplace.

Hasébé said:

'Your Izumo – the Country of the Eight-Cloud Rising† – is very distant. Perhaps it will therefore be difficult for you to promise to return here upon any particular day. But, if we were to know the exact day, we should feel happier. We could then prepare a feast of welcome; and we could watch at the gateway for your coming.'

'Why, as for that,' responded Akana, 'I have been so much accustomed to travel that I can usually tell beforehand how long it will take me to reach a place; and I can safely promise you to be here upon a particular day. Suppose we say the day of the festival Chōyō?'

---

* Related in the *Ugétsu Monogatari*.
† One of the old poetical names for the Province of Izumo, or Unshū.

'That is the ninth day of the ninth month,' said Hasébé; 'then the chrysanthemums will be in bloom, and we can go together to look at them. How pleasant! . . . So you promise to come back on the ninth day of the ninth month?'

'On the ninth day of the ninth month,' repeated Akana, smiling farewell. Then he strode away from the village of Kato in the province of Harima; and Hasébé Samon and the mother of Hasébé looked after him with tears in their eyes.

'Neither the Sun nor the Moon,' says an old Japanese proverb, 'ever halt upon their journey.' Swiftly the months went by; and the autumn came – the season of chrysanthemums. And early upon the morning of the ninth day of the ninth month Hasébé prepared to welcome his adopted brother. He made ready a feast of good things, bought wine, decorated the guest-room, and filled the vases of the alcove with chrysanthemums of two colors. Then his mother, watching him, said: 'The province of Izumo, my son, is more than one hundred *ri** from this place; and the journey thence over the mountains is difficult and weary; and you cannot be sure that Akana will be able to come to-day. Would it not be better, before you take all this trouble, to wait for his coming?' 'Nay, mother!' Hasébé made answer – 'Akana promised to be

* A *ri* is about equal to two and a half English miles.

here to-day: he could not break a promise! And if he were to see us beginning to make preparation after his arrival, he would know that we had doubted his word; and we should be put to shame.'

The day was beautiful, the sky without a cloud, and the air so pure that the world seemed to be a thousand miles wider than usual. In the morning many travellers passed through the village – some of them samurai; and Hasébé, watching each as he came, more than once imagined that he saw Akana approaching. But the temple-bells sounded the hour of midday; and Akana did not appear. Through the afternoon also Hasébé watched and waited in vain. The sun set; and still there was no sign of Akana. Nevertheless Hasébé remained at the gate, gazing down the road. Later his mother went to him, and said: 'The mind of a man, my son – as our proverb declares – may change as quickly as the sky of autumn. But your chrysanthemum-flowers will still be fresh to-morrow. Better now to sleep; and in the morning you can watch again for Akana, if you wish.' 'Rest well, mother,' returned Hasébé; 'but I still believe that he will come.' Then the mother went to her own room; and Hasébé lingered at the gate.

The night was pure as the day had been: all the sky throbbed with stars; and the white River of Heaven shimmered with unusual splendor. The village slept; the silence was broken only by the noise of a little brook, and by the far-away barking of peasants' dogs. Hasébé still waited – waited until he saw the thin moon sink behind the neighboring hills. Then at last he began to doubt and to fear. Just as he was about to re-enter the house, he perceived in the distance a tall man approaching – very lightly and quickly; and in the next moment he recognized Akana.

'Oh!' cried Hasébé, springing to meet him – 'I have been waiting for you from the morning until now! . . . So you really did keep your promise after all . . . But you must be tired, poor brother! – come in; everything is ready for you.' He guided Akana to the place of honor in the guest-room, and hastened to trim the lights, which were burning low. 'Mother,' continued Hasébé, 'felt a little tired this evening, and she has already gone to bed; but I shall awaken her presently.' Akana shook his head, and made a little gesture of disapproval. 'As you will, brother,' said Hasébé; and he set warm food and wine before the traveller. Akana did not touch the food or the wine, but remained motionless and silent for a short time. Then, speaking in a whisper – as if fearful of awakening the mother, he said:

'Now I must tell you how it happened that I came thus late. When I returned to Izumo I found that the people had almost forgotten the kindness of our former ruler, the good Lord Enya, and were seeking the favor of the usurper Tsunéhisa, who had possessed himself of the Tonda Castle. But I had to visit my cousin, Akana Tanji, though he had accepted service under Tsunéhisa, and was living, as a retainer, within the castle grounds. He persuaded me to present myself before Tsunéhisa: I yielded chiefly in order to observe the character of the new ruler, whose face I had never seen. He is a skilled soldier, and of great courage; but he is cunning and cruel. I found it necessary to let him know that I could never enter into his service. After I left his presence he ordered my cousin to detain me – to keep me confined within the house. I protested that I had promised to return to Harima upon the ninth day of the ninth month; but I was refused permission to go. I then hoped to escape from the castle at night; but I was constantly watched; and until to-day I could find no way to fulfil my promise . . .'

'Until to-day!' exclaimed Hasébé in bewilderment; 'the castle is more than a hundred *ri* from here!'

'Yes,' returned Akana; 'and no living man can travel on foot a hundred *ri* in one day. But I felt that, if I did not keep my promise, you could not think well of me; and I remembered the ancient proverb, *Tama yoku ichi nichi ni sen ri wo yuku* ['The soul of a man can journey a thousand *ri* in a day']. Fortunately I had been allowed to keep my sword; thus only was I able to come to you . . . Be good to our mother.'

With these words he stood up, and in the same instant disappeared.

Then Hasébé knew that Akana had killed himself in order to fulfil the promise.

*

At earliest dawn Hasébé Samon set out for the Castle Tonda, in the province of Izumo. Reaching Matsué, he there learned that, on the night of the ninth day of the ninth month, Akana Soyëmon had performed *harakiri* in the house of Akana Tanji, in the grounds of the castle. Then Hasébé went to the house of Akana Tanji, and reproached Akana Tanji for the treachery done, and slew him in the midst of his family, and escaped without hurt. And when the Lord Tsunéhisa had heard the story, he gave commands that Hasébé should not be pursued. For, although an unscrupulous and cruel man himself, the Lord Tsunéhisa could respect the love of truth in others, and could admire the friendship and the courage of Hasébé Samon.

Of a Promise Broken*

I

'I am not afraid to die,' said the dying wife; 'there is only one thing that troubles me now. I wish that I could know who will take my place in this house.'

'My dear one,' answered the sorrowing husband, 'nobody shall ever take your place in my home. I will never, never marry again.'

At the time that he said this he was speaking out of his heart; for he loved the woman whom he was about to lose.

'On the faith of a samurai?' she questioned, with a feeble smile.

'On the faith of a samurai,' he responded – stroking the pale thin face.

'Then, my dear one,' she said, 'you will let me be buried in the garden – will you not? – near those plum-trees that we planted at the further end? I wanted long ago to ask this; but I thought, that if you were to marry again,

* Izumo legend.

you would not like to have my grave so near you. Now you have promised that no other woman shall take my place; so I need not hesitate to speak of my wish . . . I want so much to be buried in the garden! I think that in the garden I should sometimes hear your voice, and that I should still be able to see the flowers in the spring.'

'It shall be as you wish,' he answered. 'But do not now speak of burial: you are not so ill that we have lost all hope.'

'*I* have,' she returned; 'I shall die this morning . . . But you will bury me in the garden?'

'Yes,' he said – 'under the shade of the plum-trees that we planted; and you shall have a beautiful tomb there.'

'And will you give me a little bell?'

'Bell – ?'

'Yes: I want you to put a little bell in the coffin – such a little bell as the Buddhist pilgrims carry. Shall I have it?'

'You shall have the little bell – and anything else that you wish.'

'I do not wish for anything else,' she said . . . 'My dear one, you have been very good to me always. Now I can die happy.'

Then she closed her eyes and died – as easily as a tired child falls asleep. She looked beautiful when she was dead; and there was a smile upon her face.

She was buried in the garden, under the shade of the trees that she loved; and a small bell was buried with her.

Above the grave was erected a handsome monument, decorated with the family crest, and bearing the *kaimyō*: '*Great Elder Sister, Luminous-Shadow-of-the-Plum-Flower-Chamber, dwelling in the Mansion of the Great Sea of Compassion.*'

But, within a twelve-month after the death of his wife, the relatives and friends of the samurai began to insist that he should marry again. 'You are still a young man,' they said, 'and an only son; and you have no children. It is the duty of a samurai to marry. If you die childless, who will there be to make the offerings and to remember the ancestors?'

By many such representations he was at last persuaded to marry again. The bride was only seventeen years old; and he found that he could love her dearly, notwithstanding the dumb reproach of the tomb in the garden.

II

Nothing took place to disturb the happiness of the young wife until the seventh day after the wedding – when her husband was ordered to undertake certain duties requiring his presence at the castle by night. On the first evening that he was obliged to leave her alone, she felt uneasy in a way that she could not explain – vaguely afraid without knowing why. When she went to bed she could not sleep. There was a strange oppression in the air – an indefinable heaviness like that which sometimes precedes the coming of a storm.

About the Hour of the Ox she heard, outside in the night, the clanging of a bell – a Buddhist pilgrim's bell; and she wondered what pilgrim could be passing through the samurai quarter at such a time. Presently, after a pause, the bell sounded much nearer. Evidently the pilgrim was approaching the house; but why approaching from the rear, where no road was? . . . Suddenly the dogs began to whine and howl in an unusual and horrible way; and a fear came upon her like the fear of dreams . . . That ringing was certainly in the garden . . . She tried to get up to waken a servant. But she found that she could not rise – could not move – could not call . . . And nearer, and still more near, came the clang of the bell; and oh! how the dogs howled! . . . Then, lightly as a shadow steals, there glided into the room a Woman – though every door stood fast, and every screen unmoved – a Woman robed in a grave-robe, and carrying a pilgrim's bell. Eyeless she came – because she had long been dead; and her loosened hair streamed down about her face; and she looked without eyes through the tangle of it, and spoke without a tongue:

'*Not in this house – not in this house shall you stay! Here I am mistress still. You shall go; and you shall tell to none the reason of your going. If you tell HIM, I will tear you into pieces!*'

So speaking, the haunter vanished. The bride became senseless with fear. Until the dawn she so remained.

*

Nevertheless, in the cheery light of day, she doubted the reality of what she had seen and heard. The memory of the warning still weighed upon her so heavily that she did not dare to speak of the vision, either to her husband or to any one else; but she was almost able to persuade herself that she had only dreamed an ugly dream, which had made her ill.

On the following night, however, she could not doubt. Again, at the Hour of the Ox, the dogs began to howl and whine; again the bell resounded – approaching slowly from the garden; again the listener vainly strove to rise and call; again the dead came into the room, and hissed,

'You shall go; and you shall tell to no one why you must go! If you even whisper it to HIM, I will tear you in pieces!' . . .

This time the haunter came close to the couch – and bent and muttered and mowed above it . . .

Next morning, when the samurai returned from the castle, his young wife prostrated herself before him in supplication:

'I beseech you,' she said, 'to pardon my ingratitude and my great rudeness in thus addressing you: but I want to go home; I want to go away at once.'

'Are you not happy here?' he asked, in sincere surprise. 'Has any one dared to be unkind to you during my absence?'

'It is not that –' she answered, sobbing. 'Everybody

here has been only too good to me . . . But I cannot continue to be your wife; I must go away . . .'

'My dear,' he exclaimed, in great astonishment, 'it is very painful to know that you have had any cause for unhappiness in this house. But I cannot even imagine why you should want to go away – unless somebody has been very unkind to you . . . Surely you do not mean that you wish for a divorce?'

She responded, trembling and weeping,

'If you do not give me a divorce, I shall die!'

He remained for a little while silent – vainly trying to think of some cause for this amazing declaration. Then, without betraying any emotion, he made answer:

'To send you back now to your people, without any fault on your part, would seem a shameful act. If you will tell me a good reason for your wish – any reason that will enable me to explain matters honorably – I can write you a divorce. But unless you give me a reason, a good reason, I will not divorce you – for the honor of our house must be kept above reproach.'

And then she felt obliged to speak; and she told him everything – adding, in an agony of terror –

'Now that I have let you know, she will kill me! – she will kill me! . . .'

Although a brave man, and little inclined to believe in phantoms, the samurai was more than startled for the moment. But a simple and natural explanation of the matter soon presented itself to his mind.

'My dear,' he said, 'you are now very nervous; and I fear that some one has been telling you foolish stories. I cannot give you a divorce merely because you have had a bad dream in this house. But I am very sorry indeed that you should have been suffering in such a way during my absence. To-night, also, I must be at the castle; but you shall not be alone. I will order two of the retainers to keep watch in your room; and you will be able to sleep in peace. They are good men; and they will take all possible care of you.'

Then he spoke to her so considerately and so affectionately that she became almost ashamed of her terrors, and resolved to remain in the house.

III

The two retainers left in charge of the young wife were big, brave, simple-hearted men – experienced guardians of women and children. They told the bride pleasant stories to keep her cheerful. She talked with them a long time, laughed at their good-humored fun, and almost forgot her fears. When at last she lay down to sleep, the men-at-arms took their places in a corner of the room, behind a screen, and began a game of *go** – speaking only

---

* A game resembling draughts, but much more complicated.

in whispers, that she might not be disturbed. She slept like an infant.

But again at the Hour of the Ox she awoke with a moan of terror – for she heard the bell! . . . It was already near, and was coming nearer. She started up; she screamed; but in the room there was no stir – only a silence as of death – a silence growing – a silence thickening. She rushed to the men-at-arms: they sat before their checker-table – motionless – each staring at the other with fixed eyes. She shrieked to them: she shook them: they remained as if frozen . . .

Afterwards they said that they had heard the bell – heard also the cry of the bride – even felt her try to shake them into wakefulness; and that, nevertheless, they had not been able to move or speak. From the same moment they had ceased to hear or to see: a black sleep had seized upon them.

Entering his bridal chamber at dawn, the samurai beheld, by the light of a dying lamp, the headless body of his young wife, lying in a pool of blood. Still squatting before their unfinished game, the two retainers slept. At their master's cry they sprang up, and stupidly stared at the horror on the floor . . .

The head was nowhere to be seen; and the hideous wound showed that it had not been cut off, but *torn off*. A trail of blood led from the chamber to an angle of the outer gallery, where the storm-doors appeared to have been riven apart. The three men followed that trail into the garden – over reaches of grass – over spaces of sand – along the bank of an iris-bordered pond – under heavy shadowings of cedar and bamboo. And suddenly, at a turn, they found themselves face to face with a nightmare-thing that chippered like a bat: the figure of the long-buried woman, erect before her tomb – in one hand clutching a bell, in the other the dripping head ... For a moment the three stood numbed. Then one of the men-at-arms, uttering a Buddhist invocation, drew, and struck at the shape. Instantly it crumbled down upon the soil – an empty scattering of grave-rags, bones, and hair; and the bell rolled clanking out of the ruin. But the flesh-less right hand, though parted from the wrist, still writhed; and its fingers still gripped at the bleeding head – and tore, and mangled – as the claws of the yellow crab cling fast to a fallen fruit ...

['That is a wicked story,' I said to the friend who had related it. 'The vengeance of the dead – if taken at all – should have been taken upon the man.'

'Men think so,' he made answer. 'But that is not the way that a woman feels ...'

He was right.]

Before the Supreme Court

The great Buddhist priest, Mongaku Shōnin, says in his book *Kyō-gyō Shin-shō*: 'Many of those gods whom the people worship are unjust gods [*jajin*]: therefore such gods are not worshipped by persons who revere the Three Precious Things.* And even persons who obtain favors from those gods, in answer to prayer, usually find at a later day that such favors cause misfortune.' This truth is well exemplified by a story recorded in the book *Nihon-Rei-Iki*.

During the time of the Emperor Shōmu† there lived in the district called Yamadagori, in the province of Sanuki, a man named Fushiki no Shin. He had but one child, a daughter called Kinumé.‡ Kinumé was a fine-looking girl, and very strong; but, shortly after she had reached her eighteenth year, a dangerous sickness began to prevail in that part of the country, and she was attacked by it. Her

---

* Sambō (Ratnatraya) – the Buddha, the Doctrine, and the Priesthood.
† He reigned during the second quarter of the eighth century.
‡ 'Golden Plum-Flower'.

parents and friends then made offerings on her behalf to a certain Pest-God, and performed great austerities in honor of the Pest-God – beseeching him to save her.

After having lain in a stupor for several days, the sick girl one evening came to herself, and told her parents a dream that she had dreamed. She had dreamed that the Pest-God appeared to her, and said: 'Your people have been praying to me so earnestly for you, and have been worshipping me so devoutly, that I really wish to save you. But I cannot do so except by giving you the life of some other person. Do you happen to know of any other girl who has the same name as yours?' 'I remember,' answered Kinumé, 'that in Utarigori there is a girl whose name is the same as mine.' 'Point her out to me,' the God said, touching the sleeper; and at the touch she rose into the air with him; and, in less than a second, the two were in front of the house of the other Kinumé, in Utarigori. It was night; but the family had not yet gone to bed, and the daughter was washing something in the kitchen. 'That is the girl,' said Kinumé of Yamadagori. The Pest-God took out of a scarlet bag at his girdle a long sharp instrument shaped like a chisel; and, entering the house, he drove the sharp instrument into the forehead of Kinumé of Utarigori. Then Kinumé of Utarigori sank to the floor in great agony; and Kinumé of Yamadagori awoke, and related the dream.

Immediately after having related it, however, she again fell into a stupor. For three days she remained without knowledge of the world; and her parents began to despair of her recovery. Then once more she opened her eyes, and spoke. But almost in the same moment she rose from her bed, looked wildly about the room, and rushed out of the house, exclaiming: 'This is not my home! – you are not my parents!' . . .

Something strange had happened.

Kinumé of Utarigori had died after having been stricken by the Pest-God. Her parents sorrowed greatly; and the priests of their parish-temple performed a Buddhist service for her; and her body was burned in a field outside the village. Then her spirit descended to the Meido, the world of the dead, and was summoned to the tribunal of Emma-Dai-Ō – the King and Judge of Souls. But no sooner had the Judge cast eyes upon her than he exclaimed: 'This girl is the Utarigori-Kinumé: she ought not to have been brought here so soon! Send her back at once to the *Shaba*-world,* and fetch me the other Kinumé – the Yamadagori girl!' Then the spirit of Kinumé of Utarigori made moan before King Emma, and complained, saying: 'Great Lord, it is more than three days since I died; and by this time my body must have been burned; and, if you now send me back to the *Shaba*-world, what shall I do? My body has been changed into ashes

---

* The *Shaba*-world (*Sahaloka*), in common parlance, signifies the world of men – the region of human existence.

and smoke; I shall have no body!' 'Do not be anxious,' the terrible King answered; 'I am going to give you the body of Kinumé of Yamadagori – for her spirit must be brought here to me at once. You need not fret about the burning of your body: you will find the body of the other Kinumé very much better.' And scarcely had he finished speaking when the spirit of Kinumé of Utarigori revived in the body of Kinumé of Yamadagori.

Now when the parents of Kinumé of Yamadagori saw their sick girl spring up and run away, exclaiming, 'This is not my home!' – they imagined her to be out of her mind, and they ran after her, calling out: 'Kinumé, where are you going? – wait for a moment, child! you are much too ill to run like that!' But she escaped from them, and ran on without stopping, until she came to Utarigori, and to the house of the family of the dead Kinumé. There she entered, and found the old people; and she saluted them, crying: 'Oh, how pleasant to be again at home! ... Is it well with you, dear parents?' They did not recognize her, and thought her mad; but the mother spoke to her kindly, asking: 'Where have you come from, child?' 'From the Meido I have come,' Kinumé made answer. 'I am your own child, Kinumé, returned to you from the dead. But I have now another body, mother.' And she related all that had happened; and the old people wondered exceedingly, yet did not know what to believe. Presently the parents of Kinumé of Yamadagori also came to the house, looking for their daughter; and then the two fathers and the two mothers consulted together, and made the girl repeat her story, and questioned her over and over again. But she replied to every question in such a way that the truth of her statements could not be doubted. At last the mother of the Yamadagori Kinumé, after having related the strange dream which her sick daughter had dreamed, said to the parents of the Utarigori Kinumé: 'We are satisfied that the spirit of this girl is the spirit of your child. But you know that her body is the body of our child; and we think that both families ought to have a share in her. So we would ask you to agree that she be considered henceforward the daughter of both families.' To this proposal the Utarigori parents joyfully consented; and it is recorded that in after-time Kinumé inherited the property of both households.

'This story,' says the Japanese author of the *Bukkyō-Hyakkwa-Zenshō*, 'may be found on the left side of the twelfth sheet of the first volume of the *Nihon-Rei-Iki*.'

The Story of Kwashin Koji*

During the period of Tenshō† there lived, in one of the
northern districts of Kyōto, an old man whom the people
called Kwashin Koji. He wore a long white beard, and
was always dressed like a Shintō priest; but he made his
living by exhibiting Buddhist pictures and by preaching
Buddhist doctrine. Every fine day he used to go to the
grounds of the temple Gion, and there suspend to some
tree a large *kakémono* on which were depicted the pun-
ishments of the various hells. This *kakémono* was so
wonderfully painted that all things represented in it
seemed to be real; and the old man would discourse to
the people crowding to see it, and explain to them the
Law of Cause and Effect, pointing out with a Buddhist
staff [*nyoi*], which he always carried, each detail of the
different torments, and exhorting everybody to follow
the teachings of the Buddha. Multitudes assembled to
look at the picture and to hear the old man preach about

* Related in the curious old book *Yasō-Kidan*.
† The period of Tenshō lasted from 1573 to 1591 AD. The death of the great
captain, Oda Nobunaga, who figures in this story, occurred in 1582.

it; and sometimes the mat which he spread before him, to receive contributions, was covered out of sight by the heaping of coins thrown upon it.

Oda Nobunaga was at that time ruler of Kyōto and of the surrounding provinces. One of his retainers, named Arakawa, during a visit to the temple of Gion, happened to see the picture being displayed there; and he afterwards talked about it at the palace. Nobunaga was interested by Arakawa's description, and sent orders to Kwashin Koji to come at once to the palace, and to bring the picture with him.

When Nobunaga saw the *kakémono* he was not able to conceal his surprise at the vividness of the work: the demons and the tortured spirits actually appeared to move before his eyes; and he heard voices crying out of the picture; and the blood there represented seemed to be really flowing – so that he could not help putting out his finger to feel if the painting was wet. But the finger was not stained – for the paper proved to be perfectly dry. More and more astonished, Nobunaga asked who had made the wonderful picture. Kwashin Koji answered that it had been painted by the famous Oguri Sōtan* – after he had performed the rite of self-purification every day for a hundred days, and practised great austerities,

---

* Oguri Sōtan was a great religious artist who flourished in the early part of the fifteenth century. He became a Buddhist priest in the later years of his life.

and made earnest prayer for inspiration to the divine Kwannon of Kiyomidzu Temple.

Observing Nobunaga's evident desire to possess the *kakémono*, Arakawa then asked Kwashin Koji whether he would 'offer it up', as a gift to the great lord. But the old man boldly answered: 'This painting is the only object of value that I possess; and I am able to make a little money by showing it to the people. Were I now to present this picture to the lord, I should deprive myself of the only means which I have to make my living. However, if the lord be greatly desirous to possess it, let him pay me for it the sum of one hundred *ryō* of gold. With that amount of money I should be able to engage in some profitable business. Otherwise, I must refuse to give up the picture.'

Nobunaga did not seem to be pleased at this reply; and he remained silent. Arakawa presently whispered something in the ear of the lord, who nodded assent; and Kwashin Koji was then dismissed, with a small present of money.

But when the old man left the palace, Arakawa secretly followed him – hoping for a chance to get the picture by foul means. The chance came; for Kwashin Koji happened to take a road leading directly to the heights beyond the town. When he reached a certain lonesome spot at the foot of the hills, where the road made a sudden turn, he was seized by Arakawa, who said to him: 'Why were you so greedy as to ask a hundred *ryō* of gold for that picture? Instead of a hundred *ryō* of gold, I am now going to give you one piece of iron three feet long.' Then Arakawa drew his sword, and killed the old man, and took the picture.

The next day Arakawa presented the *kakémono* – still wrapped up as Kwashin Koji had wrapped it before leaving the palace – to Oda Nobunaga, who ordered it to be hung up forthwith. But, when it was unrolled, both Nobunaga and his retainer were astounded to find that there was no picture at all – nothing but a blank surface. Arakawa could not explain how the original painting had disappeared; and as he had been guilty – whether willingly or unwillingly – of deceiving his master, it was decided that he should be punished. Accordingly he was sentenced to remain in confinement for a considerable time.

Scarcely had Arakawa completed his term of imprisonment, when news was brought to him that Kwashin Koji was exhibiting the famous picture in the grounds of Kitano Temple. Arakawa could hardly believe his ears; but the information inspired him with a vague hope that he might be able, in some way or other, to secure the *kakémono*, and thereby redeem his recent fault. So he quickly assembled some of his followers, and hurried to the temple; but when he reached it he was told that Kwashin Koji had gone away.

Several days later, word was brought to Arakawa that Kwashin Koji was exhibiting the picture at Kiyomidzu Temple, and preaching about it to an immense crowd. Arakawa made all haste to Kiyomidzu; but he arrived there only in time to see the crowd disperse – for Kwashin Koji had again disappeared.

At last one day Arakawa unexpectedly caught sight of Kwashin Koji in a wine-shop, and there captured him. The old man only laughed good-humoredly on finding himself seized, and said: 'I will go with you; but please wait until I drink a little wine.' To this request Arakawa made no objection; and Kwashin Koji thereupon drank, to the amazement of the bystanders, twelve bowls of wine. After drinking the twelfth he declared himself satisfied; and Arakawa ordered him to be bound with a rope, and taken to Nobunaga's residence.

In the court of the palace Kwashin Koji was examined at once by the Chief Officer, and sternly reprimanded. Finally the Chief Officer said to him: 'It is evident that you have been deluding people by magical practices; and for this offence alone you deserve to be heavily punished. However, if you will now respectfully offer up that picture to the Lord Nobunaga, we shall this time overlook your fault. Otherwise we shall certainly inflict upon you a very severe punishment.'

At this menace Kwashin Koji laughed in a bewildered way, and exclaimed: 'It is not I who have been guilty of deluding people.' Then, turning to Arakawa, he cried out:

'You are the deceiver! You wanted to flatter the lord by giving him that picture; and you tried to kill me in order to steal it. Surely, if there be any such thing as crime, that was a crime! As luck would have it, you did not succeed in killing me; but if you had succeeded, as you wished, what would you have been able to plead in excuse for such an act? You stole the picture, at all events. The picture that I now have is only a copy. And after you stole the picture, you changed your mind about giving it to Lord Nobunaga; and you devised a plan to keep it for yourself. So you gave a blank *kakémono* to Lord Nobunaga; and, in order to conceal your secret act and purpose, you pretended that I had deceived you by substituting a blank *kakémono* for the real one. Where the real picture now is, I do not know. You probably do.'

At these words Arakawa became so angry that he rushed towards the prisoner, and would have struck him but for the interference of the guards. And this sudden outburst of anger caused the Chief Officer to suspect that Arakawa was not altogether innocent. He ordered Kwashin Koji to be taken to prison for the time being; and he then proceeded to question Arakawa closely. Now Arakawa was naturally slow of speech; and on this occasion, being greatly excited, he could scarcely speak at all; and he stammered, and contradicted himself, and betrayed every sign of guilt. Then the Chief Officer ordered that Arakawa should be beaten with a stick until he told the truth. But it was not possible for him even to seem to tell the truth. So he was beaten with a bamboo until his senses departed from him, and he lay as if dead.

Kwashin Koji was told in the prison about what had happened to Arakawa; and he laughed. But after a little while he said to the jailer: 'Listen! That fellow Arakawa really behaved like a rascal; and I purposely brought this punishment upon him, in order to correct his evil inclinations. But now please say to the Chief Officer that Arakawa must have been ignorant of the truth, and that I shall explain the whole matter satisfactorily.'

Then Kwashin Koji was again taken before the Chief Officer, to whom he made the following declaration: 'In any picture of real excellence there must be a ghost; and such a picture, having a will of its own, may refuse to be separated from the person who gave it life, or even from its rightful owner. There are many stories to prove that really great pictures have souls. It is well known that some sparrows, painted upon a sliding-screen [*fusuma*] by Hōgen Yenshin, once flew away, leaving blank the spaces which they had occupied upon the surface. Also it is well known that a horse, painted upon a certain *kakémono*, used to go out at night to eat grass. Now, in this present case, I believe the truth to be that, inasmuch as the Lord Nobunaga never became the rightful owner of my *kakémono*, the picture voluntarily vanished from the paper when it was unrolled in his presence. But if you will give me the price that I first asked – one hundred *ryō* of gold – I think that the painting will then reappear, of its own accord, upon the now blank paper. At all events, let us try! There is nothing to risk – since, if the picture does not reappear, I shall at once return the money.'

On hearing of these strange assertions, Nobunaga ordered the hundred *ryō* to be paid, and came in person to observe the result. The *kakémono* was then unrolled before him; and, to the amazement of all present, the painting reappeared, with all its details. But the colors seemed to have faded a little; and the figures of the souls and the demons did not look really alive, as before. Perceiving this difference, the lord asked Kwashin Koji to explain the reason of it; and Kwashin Koji replied: 'The value of the painting, as you first saw it, was the value of a painting beyond all price. But the value of the painting, as you now see it, represents exactly what you paid for it – one hundred *ryō* of gold . . . How could it be otherwise?' On hearing this answer, all present felt that it would be worse than useless to oppose the old man any further. He was immediately set at liberty; and Arakawa was also liberated, as he had more than expiated his fault by the punishment which he had undergone.

Now Arakawa had a younger brother named Buichi – also a retainer in the service of Nobunaga. Buichi was furiously angry because Arakawa had been beaten and imprisoned; and he resolved to kill Kwashin Koji. Kwashin

Koji no sooner found himself again at liberty than he went straight to a wine-shop, and called for wine. Buichi rushed after him into the shop, struck him down, and cut off his head. Then, taking the hundred *ryō* that had been paid to the old man, Buichi wrapped up the head and the gold together in a cloth, and hurried home to show them to Arakawa. But when he unfastened the cloth he found, instead of the head, only an empty wine-gourd, and only a lump of filth instead of the gold . . . And the bewilderment of the brothers was presently increased by the information that the headless body had disappeared from the wine-shop – none could say how or when.

Nothing more was heard of Kwashin Koji until about a month later, when a drunken man was found one evening asleep in the gateway of Lord Nobunaga's palace, and snoring so loud that every snore sounded like the rumbling of distant thunder. A retainer discovered that the drunkard was Kwashin Koji. For this insolent offence, the old fellow was at once seized and thrown into the prison. But he did not awake; and in the prison he continued to sleep without interruption for ten days and ten nights – all the while snoring so that the sound could be heard to a great distance.

About this time, the Lord Nobunaga came to his death through the treachery of one of his captains, Akéchi

Mitsuhidé, who thereupon usurped rule. But Mitsuhidé's power endured only for a period of twelve days.

Now when Mitsuhidé became master of Kyōto, he was told of the case of Kwashin Koji; and he ordered that the prisoner should be brought before him. Accordingly Kwashin Koji was summoned into the presence of the new lord; but Mitsuhidé spoke to him kindly, treated him as a guest, and commanded that a good dinner should be served to him. When the old man had eaten, Mitsuhidé said to him: 'I have heard that you are very fond of wine; how much wine can you drink at a single sitting?' Kwashin Koji answered: 'I do not really know how much; I stop drinking only when I feel intoxication coming on.' Then the lord set a great wine-cup* before Kwashin Koji, and told a servant to fill the cup as often as the old man wished. And Kwashin Koji emptied the great cup ten times in succession, and asked for more; but the servant made answer that the wine-vessel was exhausted. All present were astounded by this drinking-feat; and the lord asked Kwashin Koji, 'Are you not yet satisfied, Sir?' 'Well, yes,' replied Kwashin Koji, 'I am somewhat satisfied; and now, in return for your august kindness, I shall display a little of my art. Be therefore so good as to observe that

* The term 'bowl' would better indicate the kind of vessel to which the story-teller refers. Some of the so-called cups, used on festival occasions, were very large – shallow lacquered basins capable of holding considerably more than a quart. To empty one of the largest size, at a draught, was considered to be no small feat.

screen.' He pointed to a large eight-folding screen upon which were painted the Eight Beautiful Views of the Lake of Ōmi (*Ōmi-Hakkei*); and everybody looked at the screen. In one of the views the artist had represented, far away on the lake, a man rowing a boat – the boat occupying, upon the surface of the screen, a space of less than an inch in length. Kwashin Koji then waved his hand in the direction of the boat; and all saw the boat suddenly turn, and begin to move toward the foreground of the picture. It grew rapidly larger and larger as it approached; and presently the features of the boatman became clearly distinguishable. Still the boat drew nearer – always becoming larger – until it appeared to be only a short distance away. And, all of a sudden, the water of the lake seemed to overflow – out of the picture into the room; – and the room was flooded; and the spectators girded up their robes in haste, as the water rose above their knees. In the same moment the boat appeared to glide out of the screen – a real fishing-boat; and the creaking of the single oar could be heard. Still the flood in the room continued to rise, until the spectators were standing up to their girdles in water. Then the boat came close up to Kwashin Koji; and Kwashin Koji climbed into it; and the boatman turned about, and began to row away very swiftly. And, as the boat receded, the water in the room began to lower rapidly – seeming to ebb back into the screen. No sooner had the boat passed the apparent foreground of the picture than the room was dry again! But still the painted vessel appeared to glide over the painted water – retreating further into the distance, and ever growing smaller – till at last it dwindled to a dot in the offing. And then it disappeared altogether; and Kwashin Koji disappeared with it. He was never again seen in Japan.

In a Cup of Tea

Have you ever attempted to mount some old tower stair-way, spiring up through darkness, and in the heart of that darkness found yourself at the cobwebbed edge of noth-ing? Or have you followed some coast path, cut along the face of a cliff, only to discover yourself, at a turn, on the jagged verge of a break. The emotional worth of such experience – from a literary point of view – is proved by the force of the sensations aroused, and by the vividness with which they are remembered.

Now there have been curiously preserved, in old Japa-nese story-books, certain fragments of fiction that produce an almost similar emotional experience . . . Perhaps the writer was lazy; perhaps he had a quarrel with the pub-lisher; perhaps he was suddenly called away from his little table, and never came back; perhaps death stopped the writing-brush in the very middle of a sentence.

But no mortal man can ever tell us exactly why these things were left unfinished . . . I select a typical example.

On the fourth day of the first month of the third Tenwa, – that is to say, about two hundred and twenty years ago, – the lord Nakagawa Sado, while on his way to make a New Year's visit, halted with his train at a tea-house in Hakusan, in the Hongō district of Yedo. While the party were resting there, one of the lord's attendants – a *wakatō** named Sekinai – feeling very thirsty, filled for himself a large water-cup with tea. He was raising the cup to his lips when he suddenly perceived, in the transparent yellow infusion, the image or reflection of a face that was not his own. Startled, he looked around, but could see no one near him. The face in the tea appeared, from the coiffure, to be the face of a young samurai: it was strangely distinct, and very handsome – delicate as the face of a girl. And it seemed the reflection of a living face; for the eyes and the lips were moving. Bewildered by this mysterious apparition, Sekinai threw away the tea, and carefully examined the cup. It proved to be a very cheap water-cup, with no artistic devices of any sort. He found and filled another cup; and again the face appeared in the tea. He then ordered fresh tea, and refilled the cup; and once more the strange face appeared – this time with a mocking smile. But Sekinai did not allow himself to be frightened. 'Whoever you are,' he muttered, 'you shall delude me no further!' – then he swallowed the tea, face

---

* The armed attendant of a samurai was thus called. The relation of the *wakatō* to the samurai was that of squire to knight.

and all, and went his way, wondering whether he had swallowed a ghost.

Late in the evening of the same day, while on watch in the palace of the lord Nakagawa, Sekinai was surprised by the soundless coming of a stranger into the apartment. This stranger, a richly dressed young samurai, seated himself directly in front of Sekinai, and, saluting the *wakatō* with a slight bow, observed:

'I am Shikibu Heinai – met you to-day for the first time . . . You do not seem to recognize me.'

He spoke in a very low, but penetrating voice. And Sekinai was astonished to find before him the same sinister, handsome face of which he had seen, and swallowed, the apparition in a cup of tea. It was smiling now, as the phantom had smiled; but the steady gaze of the eyes, above the smiling lips, was at once a challenge and an insult.

'No, I do not recognize you,' returned Sekinai, angry but cool; 'and perhaps you will now be good enough to inform me how you obtained admission to this house?'

[In feudal times the residence of a lord was strictly guarded at all hours; and no one could enter unannounced, except through some unpardonable negligence on the part of the armed watch.]

'Ah, you do not recognize me!' exclaimed the visitor, in a tone of irony, drawing a little nearer as he spoke. 'No, you do not recognize me! Yet you took upon yourself this morning to do me a deadly injury! . . .'

Sekinai instantly seized the *tantō** at his girdle, and made a fierce thrust at the throat of the man. But the blade seemed to touch no substance. Simultaneously and soundlessly the intruder leaped sideward to the chamber-wall, *and through it!* . . . The wall showed no trace of his exit. He had traversed it only as the light of a candle passes through lantern-paper.

When Sekinai made report of the incident, his recital astonished and puzzled the retainers. No stranger had been seen either to enter or to leave the palace at the hour of the occurrence; and no one in the service of the lord Nakagawa had ever heard of the name 'Shikibu Heinai'.

On the following night Sekinai was off duty, and remained at home with his parents. At a rather late hour he was informed that some strangers had called at the house, and desired to speak with him for a moment. Taking his sword, he went to the entrance, and there found three armed men – apparently retainers – waiting in front of the doorstep. The three bowed respectfully to Sekinai; and one of them said:

'Our names are Matsuoka Bungō, Tsuchibashi Bungō,

---

* The shorter of the two swords carried by samurai. The longer sword was called *katana*.

and Okamura Heiroku. We are retainers of the noble Shi-kibu Heinai. When our master last night deigned to pay you a visit, you struck him with a sword. He was much hurt, and has been obliged to go to the hot springs, where his wound is now being treated. But on the sixteenth day of the coming month he will return; and he will then fitly repay you for the injury done him . . .'

Without waiting to hear more, Sekinai leaped out, sword in hand, and slashed right and left, at the strangers. But the three men sprang to the wall of the adjoining building, and flitted up the wall like shadows, and . . .

Here the old narrative breaks off; the rest of the story existed only in some brain that has been dust for a century.

I am able to imagine several possible endings; but none of them would satisfy an Occidental imagination. I prefer to let the reader attempt to decide for himself the probable consequence of swallowing a Soul.

The Story of Chūgorō

A long time ago there lived, in the Koishikawa quarter of Yedo, a *hatamoto* named Suzuki, whose *yashiki* was situated on the bank of the Yedogawa, not far from the bridge called Naka-no-hashi. And among the retainers of this Suzuki there was an *ashigaru** named Chūgorō. Chūgorō was a handsome lad, very amiable and clever, and much liked by his comrades.

For several years Chūgorō remained in the service of Suzuki, conducting himself so well that no fault was found with him. But at last the other *ashigaru* discovered that Chūgorō was in the habit of leaving the *yashiki* every night, by way of the garden, and staying out until a little before dawn. At first they said nothing to him about this strange behaviour; for his absences did not interfere with any regular duty, and were supposed to be caused by some love-affair. But after a time he began to look pale and weak; and his comrades, suspecting some serious folly, decided to interfere. Therefore, one evening, just as

---

* The *ashigaru* were the lowest class of retainers in military service.

he was about to steal away from the house, an elderly retainer called him aside, and said:

'Chūgorō, my lad, we know that you go out every night and stay away until early morning; and we have observed that you are looking unwell. We fear that you are keeping bad company, and injuring your health. And unless you can give a good reason for your conduct, we shall think that it is our duty to report this matter to the Chief Officer. In any case, since we are your comrades and friends, it is but right that we should know why you go out at night, contrary to the custom of this house.'

Chūgorō appeared to be very much embarrassed and alarmed by these words. But after a short silence he passed into the garden, followed by his comrade. When the two found themselves well out of hearing of the rest, Chūgorō stopped, and said:

'I will now tell you everything; but I must entreat you to keep my secret. If you repeat what I tell you, some great misfortune may befall me.

'It was in the early part of last spring – about five months ago – that I first began to go out at night, on account of a love-affair. One evening, when I was returning to the *yashiki* after a visit to my parents, I saw a woman standing by the riverside, not far from the main gateway. She was dressed like a person of high rank; and I thought it strange that a woman so finely dressed should be standing there alone at such an hour. But I did not think that I had any right to question her; and I was about to pass her by, without speaking, when she stepped forward and pulled me by the sleeve. Then I saw that she was very young and handsome. "Will you not walk with me as far as the bridge?" she said; "I have something to tell you." Her voice was very soft and pleasant; and she smiled as she spoke; and her smile was hard to resist. So I walked with her toward the bridge; and on the way she told me that she had often seen me going in and out of the *yashiki*, and had taken a fancy to me. "I wish to have you for my husband," she said; "if you can like me, we shall be able to make each other very happy." I did not know how to answer her; but I thought her very charming. As we neared the bridge, she pulled my sleeve again, and led me down the bank to the very edge of the river. "Come in with me," she whispered, and pulled me toward the water. It is deep there, as you know; and I became all at once afraid of her, and tried to turn back. She smiled, and caught me by the wrist, and said, "Oh, you must never be afraid with me!" And, somehow, at the touch of her hand, I became more helpless than a child. I felt like a person in a dream who tries to run, and cannot move hand or foot. Into the deep water she stepped, and drew me with her; and I neither saw nor heard nor felt anything more until I found myself walking beside her through what seemed to be a great palace, full of light. I was neither wet nor cold: everything around me was dry and warm and beautiful. I could not understand where I was, nor how I had come there. The woman led me by the hand: we passed through room after room – through ever so many rooms, all empty, but very fine – until we entered into a guest-room of a thousand mats. Before a great alcove, at the farther end, lights were burning, and cushions laid as for a feast; but I saw no guests. She led me to the place of honor, by the alcove, and seated herself in front of me, and said: "This is my home: do you think that you could be happy with me here?" As she asked the question she smiled; and I thought that her smile was more beautiful than anything else in the world; and out of my heart I answered, "Yes . . ." In the same moment I remembered the story of Urashima; and I imagined that she might be the daughter of a god; but I feared to ask her any questions . . . Presently maid-servants came in, bearing rice-wine and many dishes, which they set before us. Then she who sat before me said: "To-night shall be our bridal night, because you like me; and this is our wedding-feast." We pledged ourselves to each other for the time of seven existences; and after the banquet we were conducted to a bridal chamber, which had been prepared for us.

'It was yet early in the morning when she awoke me, and said: "My dear one, you are now indeed my husband. But for reasons which I cannot tell you, and which you must not ask, it is necessary that our marriage remain secret. To keep you here until daybreak would cost both of us our lives. Therefore do not, I beg of you, feel displeased because I must now send you back to the house of your lord. You can come to me to-night again, and every night hereafter, at the same hour that we first met. Wait always for me by the bridge; and you will not have to wait long. But remember, above all things, that our marriage must be a secret, and that, if you talk about it, we shall probably be separated forever."

'I promised to obey her in all things – remembering the fate of Urashima – and she conducted me through many rooms, all empty and beautiful, to the entrance. There she again took me by the wrist, and everything suddenly became dark, and I knew nothing more until I found myself standing alone on the river bank, close to the Naka-no-hashi. When I got back to the *yashiki*, the temple bells had not yet begun to ring.

'In the evening I went again to the bridge, at the hour she had named, and I found her waiting for me. She took me with her, as before, into the deep water, and into the wonderful place where we had passed our bridal night. And every night, since then, I have met and parted from her in the same way. To-night she will certainly be waiting for me, and I would rather die than disappoint her: therefore I must go ... But let me again entreat you, my friend, never to speak to any one about what I have told you.'

The elder *ashigaru* was surprised and alarmed by this story. He felt that Chūgorō had told him the truth; and the truth suggested unpleasant possibilities. Probably the whole experience was an illusion, and an illusion produced by some evil power for a malevolent end. Nevertheless, if really bewitched, the lad was rather to be pitied than blamed; and any forcible interference would be likely to result in mischief. So the *ashigaru* answered kindly:

'I shall never speak of what you have told me – never, at least, while you remain alive and well. Go and meet the woman; but – beware of her! I fear that you are being deceived by some wicked spirit.'

Chūgorō only smiled at the old man's warning, and hastened away. Several hours later he re-entered the *yashiki*, with a strangely dejected look. 'Did you meet her?' whispered his comrade. 'No,' replied Chūgorō; 'she was not there. For the first time, she was not there. I think that she will never meet me again. I did wrong to tell you; I was very foolish to break my promise . . .' The other vainly tried to console him. Chūgorō lay down, and spoke no word more. He was trembling from head to foot, as if he had caught a chill.

When the temple bells announced the hour of dawn, Chūgorō tried to get up, and fell back senseless. He was evidently sick – deathly sick. A Chinese physician was summoned.

'Why, the man has no blood!' exclaimed the doctor, after a careful examination; 'there is nothing but water in his veins! It will be very difficult to save him . . . What maleficence is this?'

*

Everything was done that could be done to save Chūgorō's life – but in vain. He died as the sun went down. Then his comrade related the whole story.

'Ah! I might have suspected as much!' exclaimed the doctor . . . 'No power could have saved him. He was not the first whom she destroyed.'

'Who is she? – or what is she?' the *ashigaru* asked – 'a Fox-Woman?'

'No; she has been haunting this river from ancient time. She loves the blood of the young . . .'

'A Serpent-Woman? – A Dragon-Woman?'

'No, no! If you were to see her under that bridge by daylight, she would appear to you a very loathsome creature.'

'But what kind of a creature?'

'Simply a Frog – a great and ugly Frog!'

The Story of Mimi-nashi-Hōïchi

More than seven hundred years ago, at Dan-no-ura, in the Straits of Shimonoséki, was fought the last battle of the long contest between the Heiké, or Taira clan, and the Genji, or Minamoto clan. There the Heiké perished utterly, with their women and children, and their infant emperor likewise – now remembered as Antoku Tennō. And that sea and shore have been haunted for seven hundred years ... Elsewhere I told you about the strange crabs found there, called Heiké crabs, which have human faces on their backs, and are said to be the spirits of the Heiké warriors.* But there are many strange things to be seen and heard along that coast. On dark nights thousands of ghostly fires hover about the beach, or flit above the waves – pale lights which the fishermen call *Oni-bi*, or demon-fires; and, whenever the winds are up, a sound of great shouting comes from that sea, like a clamor of battle.

In former years the Heiké were much more restless than they now are. They would rise about ships passing

* See my *Kottō*, for a description of these curious crabs.

131

in the night, and try to sink them; and at all times they would watch for swimmers, to pull them down. It was in order to appease those dead that the Buddhist temple, Amidaji, was built at Akamagaséki.* A cemetery also was made close by, near the beach; and within it were set up monuments inscribed with the names of the drowned emperor and of his great vassals; and Buddhist services were regularly performed there, on behalf of the spirits of them. After the temple had been built, and the tombs erected, the Heiké gave less trouble than before; but they continued to do queer things at intervals – proving that they had not found the perfect peace.

Some centuries ago there lived at Akamagaséki a blind man named Hōïchi, who was famed for his skill in recitation and in playing upon the *biwa*.† From childhood he had been trained to recite and to play; and while yet a lad he had surpassed his teachers. As a professional *biwa-hōshi* he became famous chiefly by his recitations of the history of the Heiké and the Genji; and it is said that when he

---

* Or, Simonoséki. The town is also known by the name of Bakkan.
† The *biwa*, a kind of four-stringed lute, is chiefly used in musical recitative. Formerly the professional minstrels who recited the *Heiké-Monogatari*, and other tragical histories, were called *biwa-hōshi*, or 'lute-priests'. The origin of this appellation is not clear; but it is possible that it may have been suggested by the fact that 'lute-priests', as well as blind shampooers, had their heads shaven, like Buddhist priests. The *biwa* is played with a kind of plectrum, called *bachi*, usually made of horn.

sang the song of the battle of Dan-no-ura 'even the goblins [*kijin*] could not refrain from tears'.

At the outset of his career, Hōïchi was very poor; but he found a good friend to help him. The priest of the Amidaji was fond of poetry and music; and he often invited Hōïchi to the temple, to play and recite. Afterwards, being much impressed by the wonderful skill of the lad, the priest proposed that Hōïchi should make the temple his home; and this offer was gratefully accepted. Hōïchi was given a room in the temple-building; and, in return for food and lodging, he was required only to gratify the priest with a musical performance on certain evenings, when otherwise disengaged.

One summer night the priest was called away, to perform a Buddhist service at the house of a dead parishioner; and he went there with his acolyte, leaving Hōïchi alone in the temple. It was a hot night; and the blind man sought to cool himself on the verandah before his sleeping-room. The verandah overlooked a small garden in the rear of the Amidaji. There Hōïchi waited for the priest's return, and tried to relieve his solitude by practicing upon his *biwa*. Midnight passed; and the priest did not appear. But the atmosphere was still too warm for comfort within doors; and Hōïchi remained outside. At last he heard steps approaching from the back gate. Somebody crossed the garden, advanced to the verandah, and halted directly in front of him – but it was not the priest. A deep voice called the blind man's name – abruptly and unceremoniously, in the manner of a samurai summoning an inferior:

'Hōïchi!'

Hōïchi was too much startled, for the moment, to respond; and the voice called again, in a tone of harsh command,

'Hōïchi!'

'*Hai!*' answered the blind man, frightened by the menace in the voice – 'I am blind! – I cannot know who calls!'

'There is nothing to fear,' the stranger exclaimed, speaking more gently. 'I am stopping near this temple, and have been sent to you with a message. My present lord, a person of exceedingly high rank, is now staying in Akamagaséki, with many noble attendants. He wished to view the scene of the battle of Dan-no-ura; and to-day he visited that place. Having heard of your skill in reciting the story of the battle, he now desires to hear your performance: so you will take your *biwa* and come with me at once to the house where the august assembly is waiting.'

In those times, the order of a samurai was not to be lightly disobeyed. Hōïchi donned his sandals, took his *biwa*, and went away with the stranger, who guided him deftly, but obliged him to walk very fast. The hand that guided was iron; and the clank of the warrior's stride proved him fully armed – probably some palace-guard on duty. Hōïchi's first alarm was over: he began to imagine himself in good luck; for, remembering the retainer's assurance about a 'person of exceedingly high rank', he thought that the lord who wished to hear the recitation could not be less than a *daimyō* of the first class. Presently the samurai halted; and Hōïchi became aware that they had arrived at a large gateway; and he wondered, for he could not remember any large gate in that part of the town, except the main gate of the Amidaji. '*Kaimon!*'* the samurai called – and there was a sound of unbarring; and the twain passed on. They traversed a space of garden, and halted again before some entrance; and the retainer cried in a loud voice, 'Within there! I have brought Hōïchi.' Then came sounds of feet hurrying, and screens sliding, and rain-doors opening, and voices of women in converse. By the language of the women Hōïchi knew them to be domestics in some noble household; but he could not imagine to what place he had been conducted. Little time was allowed him for conjecture. After he had been helped to mount several stone steps, upon the last of which he was told to leave his sandals, a woman's hand guided him along interminable reaches of polished planking, and round pillared angles too many to remember, and over widths amazing of matted floor – into the middle of some vast apartment. There he thought that many great people were assembled: the sound of the

---

* A respectful term, signifying the opening of a gate. It was used by samurai when calling to the guards on duty at a lord's gate for admission.

rustling of silk was like the sound of leaves in a forest. He heard also a great humming of voices – talking in undertones; and the speech was the speech of courts. Hōïchi was told to put himself at ease, and he found a kneeling-cushion ready for him. After having taken his place upon it, and tuned his instrument, the voice of a woman – whom he divined to be the *Rōjo*, or matron in charge of the female service – addressed him, saying,

'It is now required that the history of the Heiké be recited, to the accompaniment of the *biwa*.'

Now the entire recital would have required a time of many nights: therefore Hōïchi ventured a question:

'As the whole of the story is not soon told, what portion is it augustly desired that I now recite?'

The woman's voice made answer:

'Recite the story of the battle at Dan-no-ura – for the pity of it is the most deep.'*

Then Hōïchi lifted up his voice, and chanted the chant of the fight on the bitter sea – wonderfully making his *biwa* to sound like the straining of oars and the rushing of ships, the whirr and the hissing of arrows, the shouting and trampling of men, the crashing of steel upon helmets, the plunging of slain in the flood. And to left and right of him, in the pauses of his playing, he could hear voices murmuring praise: 'How marvelous an artist!' – 'Never

---

* Or the phrase might be rendered, 'for the pity of that part is the deepest'. The Japanese word for pity in the original text is *awaré*.

in our own province was playing heard like this!' – 'Not in all the empire is there another singer like Hōïchi!' Then fresh courage came to him, and he played and sang yet better than before; and a hush of wonder deepened about him. But when at last he came to tell the fate of the fair and helpless – the piteous perishing of the women and children – and the death-leap of Nii-no-Ama, with the imperial infant in her arms – then all the listeners uttered together one long, long shuddering cry of anguish; and thereafter they wept and wailed so loudly and so wildly that the blind man was frightened by the violence and grief that he had made. For much time the sobbing and the wailing continued. But gradually the sounds of lamentation died away; and again, in the great stillness that followed, Hōïchi heard the voice of the woman whom he supposed to be the *Rōjo*.

She said:

'Although we had been assured that you were a very skillful player upon the *biwa*, and without an equal in recitative, we did not know that any one could be so skillful as you have proved yourself to-night. Our lord has been pleased to say that he intends to bestow upon you a fitting reward. But he desires that you shall perform before him once every night for the next six nights – after which time he will probably make his august return-journey. To-morrow night, therefore, you are to come here at the same hour. The retainer who to-night conducted you will be sent for you . . . There is another matter about which I have been

ordered to inform you. It is required that you shall speak
to no one of your visits here, during the time of our lord's
august sojourn at Akamagaséki. As he is traveling incognito,*
he commands that no mention of these things be made . . .
You are now free to go back to your temple.'

After Hōïchi had duly expressed his thanks, a woman's
hand conducted him to the entrance of the house, where
the same retainer, who had before guided him, was waiting to take him home. The retainer led him to the verandah
at the rear of the temple, and there bade him farewell.

It was almost dawn when Hōïchi returned; but his absence
from the temple had not been observed – as the priest,
coming back at a very late hour, had supposed him asleep.
During the day Hōïchi was able to take some rest; and
he said nothing about his strange adventure. In the middle of the following night the samurai again came for him,
and led him to the august assembly, where he gave
another recitation with the same success that had attended
his previous performance. But during this second visit
his absence from the temple was accidentally discovered;
and after his return in the morning he was summoned to
the presence of the priest, who said to him, in a tone of
kindly reproach:

'We have been very anxious about you, friend Hōïchi.

* 'Traveling incognito' is at least the meaning of the original phrase –
'making a disguised august-journey' (*shinobi no go-ryokō*).

To go out, blind and alone, at so late an hour, is dangerous. Why did you go without telling us? I could have ordered a servant to accompany you. And where have you been?'

Hōïchi answered, evasively,

'Pardon me, kind friend! I had to attend to some private business; and I could not arrange the matter at any other hour.'

The priest was surprised, rather than pained, by Hōïchi's reticence: he felt it to be unnatural, and suspected something wrong. He feared that the blind lad had been bewitched or deluded by some evil spirits. He did not ask any more questions; but he privately instructed the men-servants of the temple to keep watch upon Hōïchi's movements, and to follow him in case that he should again leave the temple after dark.

On the very next night, Hōïchi was seen to leave the temple; and the servants immediately lighted their lanterns, and followed after him. But it was a rainy night, and very dark; and before the temple-folks could get to the roadway, Hōïchi had disappeared. Evidently he had walked very fast – a strange thing, considering his blindness; for the road was in a bad condition. The men hurried through the streets, making inquiries at every house which Hōïchi was accustomed to visit; but nobody could give them any news of him. At last, as they were returning to the temple by way of the shore, they were startled by the sound of a *biwa*, furiously played, in the cemetery of the Amidaji.

Except for some ghostly fires – such as usually flitted there on dark nights – all was blackness in that direction. But the men at once hastened to the cemetery; and there, by the help of their lanterns, they discovered Hōïchi – sitting alone in the rain before the memorial tomb of Antoku Tennō, making his *biwa* resound, and loudly chanting the chant of the battle of Dan-no-ura. And behind him, and about him, and everywhere above the tombs, the fires of the dead were burning, like candles. Never before had so great a host of *Oni-bi* appeared in the sight of mortal man . . .

'Hōïchi San! – Hōïchi San!' the servants cried – 'you are bewitched! . . . Hōïchi San!'

But the blind man did not seem to hear. Strenuously he made his *biwa* to rattle and ring and clang; more and more wildly he chanted the chant of the battle of Dan-no-ura. They caught hold of him; they shouted into his ear,

'Hōïchi San! – Hōïchi San! – come home with us at once!'

Reprovingly he spoke to them:

'To interrupt me in such a manner, before this august assembly, will not be tolerated.'

Whereat, in spite of the weirdness of the thing, the servants could not help laughing. Sure that he had been bewitched, they now seized him, and pulled him up on his feet, and by main force hurried him back to the temple – where he was immediately relieved of his wet clothes, by order of the priest. Then the priest insisted upon a full explanation of his friend's astonishing behavior. Hōïchi long hesitated to speak. But at last, finding that his conduct had really alarmed and angered the good priest, he decided to abandon his reserve; and he related everything that had happened from the time of first visit of the samurai.

The priest said:

'Hōïchi, my poor friend, you are now in great danger! How unfortunate that you did not tell me all this before! Your wonderful skill in music has indeed brought you into strange trouble. By this time you must be aware that you have not been visiting any house whatever, but have been passing your nights in the cemetery, among the tombs of the Heiké; and it was before the memorial-tomb of Antoku Tennō that our people to-night found you, sitting in the rain. All that you have been imagining was illusion – except the calling of the dead. By once obeying them, you have put yourself in their power. If you obey them again, after what has already occurred, they will tear you in pieces. But they would have destroyed you, sooner or later, in any event . . . Now I shall not be able to remain with you to-night: I am called away to perform another service. But, before I go, it will be necessary to protect your body by writing holy texts upon it.'

Before sundown the priest and his acolyte stripped Hōïchi: then, with their writing-brushes, they traced upon

141

his breast and back, head and face and neck, limbs and hands and feet – even upon the soles of his feet, and upon all parts of his body – the text of the holy sûtra called *Hannya-Shin-Kyo*.* When this had been done, the priest instructed Hōïchi, saying:

'To-night, as soon as I go away, you must seat yourself on the verandah, and wait. You will be called. But, whatever may happen, do not answer, and do not move. Say nothing and sit still – as if meditating. If you stir, or make any noise, you will be torn asunder. Do not get frightened; and do not think of calling for help – because no help could save you. If you do exactly as I tell you, the danger will pass, and you will have nothing more to fear.'

After dark the priest and the acolyte went away; and Hōïchi seated himself on the verandah, according to the

* The Smaller Pragña-Pâramitâ-Hridaya-Sûtra is thus called in Japanese. Both the smaller and larger sûtras called Pragña-Pâramitâ ('Transcendent Wisdom') have been translated by the late Professor Max Müller, and can be found in volume xlix of the *Sacred Books of the East* ('Buddhist Mahâyâna Sûtras'). Apropos of the magical use of the text, as described in this story, it is worth remarking that the subject of the sûtra is the Doctrine of the Emptiness of Forms – that is to say, of the unreal character of all phenomena or noumena . . . 'Form is emptiness; and emptiness is form. Emptiness is not different from form; form is not different from emptiness. What is form – that is emptiness. What is emptiness – that is form . . . Perception, name, concept, and knowledge, are also emptiness . . . There is no eye, ear, nose, tongue, body, and mind. But when the envelopment of consciousness has been annihilated, then he [*the seeker*] becomes free from all fear, and beyond the reach of change, enjoying final Nirvâna.'

instructions given him. He laid his *biwa* on the planking beside him, and, assuming the attitude of meditation, remained quite still – taking care not to cough, or to breathe audibly. For hours he stayed thus.

Then, from the roadway, he heard the steps coming. They passed the gate, crossed the garden, approached the verandah, stopped – directly in front of him.

'Hōïchi!' the deep voice called. But the blind man held his breath, and sat motionless. 'Hōïchi!' grimly called the voice a second time. Then a third time – savagely:

'Hōïchi!'

Hōïchi remained as still as a stone – and the voice grumbled:

'No answer! – that won't do! . . . Must see where the fellow is.' . . .

There was a noise of heavy feet mounting upon the verandah. The feet approached deliberately – halted beside him. Then, for long minutes – during which Hōïchi felt his whole body shake to the beating of his heart – there was dead silence.

At last the gruff voice muttered close to him:

'Here is the *biwa*; but of the biwa-player I see – only two ears! . . . So that explains why he did not answer: he had no mouth to answer with – there is nothing left of him but his ears . . . Now to my lord those ears I will take – in proof that the august commands have been obeyed, so far as was possible.' . . .

At that instant Hōïchi felt his ears gripped by fingers of

iron, and torn off! Great as the pain was, he gave no cry. The heavy footfalls receded along the verandah – descended into the garden – passed out to the roadway – ceased. From either side of his head, the blind man felt a thick warm trickling; but he dared not lift his hands . . .

Before sunrise the priest came back. He hastened at once to the verandah in the rear, stepped and slipped upon something clammy, and uttered a cry of horror; for he saw, by the light of his lantern, that the clamminess was blood. But he perceived Hōïchi sitting there, in the attitude of meditation – with the blood still oozing from his wounds.

'My poor Hōïchi!' cried the startled priest – 'what is this? . . . You have been hurt?'

At the sound of his friend's voice, the blind man felt safe. He burst out sobbing, and tearfully told his adventure of the night.

'Poor, poor Hōïchi!' the priest exclaimed – 'all my fault! – my very grievous fault! . . . Everywhere upon your body the holy texts had been written – except upon your ears! I trusted my acolyte to do that part of the work; and it was very, very wrong of me not to have made sure that he had done it! . . . Well, the matter cannot now be helped; we can only try to heal your hurts as soon as possible . . . Cheer up, friend! – the danger is now well over. You will never again be troubled by those visitors.'

*

With the aid of a good doctor, Hōïchi soon recovered from his injuries. The story of his strange adventure spread far and wide, and soon made him famous. Many noble persons went to Akamagaséki to hear him recite; and large presents of money were given to him – so that he became a wealthy man ... But from the time of his adventure, he was known only by the appellation of *Mimi-nashi-Hōïchi*: 'Hōïchi-the-Earless'.

Jikininki

Once, when Musō Kokushi, a priest of the Zen sect, was journeying alone through the province of Mino, he lost his way in a mountain-district where there was nobody to direct him. For a long time he wandered about helplessly; and he was beginning to despair of finding shelter for the night, when he perceived, on the top of a hill lighted by the last rays of the sun, one of those little hermitages, called *anjitsu*, which are built for solitary priests. It seemed to be in ruinous condition; but he hastened to it eagerly, and found that it was inhabited by an aged priest, from whom he begged the favor of a night's lodging. This the old man harshly refused; but he directed Musō to a certain hamlet, in the valley adjoining where lodging and food could be obtained.

Musō found his way to the hamlet, which consisted of less than a dozen farm-cottages; and he was kindly received at the dwelling of the headman. Forty or fifty persons were assembled in the principal apartment, at the moment of Musō's arrival; but he was shown into a small separate room, where he was promptly supplied with food and bedding. Being very tired, he lay down to rest at an early hour; but a little before midnight he was roused from sleep by a sound of loud weeping in the next apartment. Presently the sliding-screens were gently pushed apart; and a young man, carrying a lighted lantern, entered the room, respectfully saluted him, and said:

'Reverend Sir, it is my painful duty to tell you that I am now the responsible head of this house. Yesterday I was only the eldest son. But when you came here, tired as you were, we did not wish that you should feel embarrassed in any way: therefore we did not tell you that father had died only a few hours before. The people whom you saw in the next room are the inhabitants of this village: they all assembled here to pay their last respects to the dead; and now they are going to another village, about three miles off – for by our custom, no one of us may remain in this village during the night after a death has taken place. We make the proper offerings and prayers; then we go away, leaving the corpse alone. Strange things always happen in the house where a corpse has thus been left: so we think that it will be better for you to come away with us. We can find you good lodging in the other village. But perhaps, as you are a priest, you have no fear of demons or evil spirits; and, if you are not afraid of being left alone with the body, you will be very welcome to the use of this poor house. However, I must tell you that nobody, except a priest, would dare to remain here to-night.'

Musō made answer:

'For your kind intention and your generous hospitality, I am deeply grateful. But I am sorry that you did not tell me of your father's death when I came; for, though I was a little tired, I certainly was not so tired that I should have found difficulty in doing my duty as a priest. Had you told me, I could have performed the service before your departure. As it is, I shall perform the service after you have gone away; and I shall stay by the body until morning. I do not know what you mean by your words about the danger of staying here alone; but I am not afraid of ghosts or demons: therefore please to feel no anxiety on my account.'

The young man appeared to be rejoiced by these assurances, and expressed his gratitude in fitting words. Then the other members of the family, and the folk assembled in the adjoining room, having been told of the priest's kind promises, came to thank him – after which the master of the house said:

'Now, reverend Sir, much as we regret to leave you alone, we must bid you farewell. By the rule of our village, none of us can stay here after midnight. We beg, kind Sir, that you will take every care of your honorable body, while we are unable to attend upon you. And if you happen to hear or see anything strange during our absence, please tell us of the matter when we return in the morning.'

*

All then left the house, except the priest, who went to the room where the dead body was lying. The usual offerings had been set before the corpse; and a small Buddhist lamp – *tōmyō* – was burning. The priest recited the service, and performed the funeral ceremonies – after which he entered into meditation. So meditating he remained through several silent hours; and there was no sound in the deserted village. But, when the hush of the night was at its deepest, there noiselessly entered a Shape, vague and vast; and in the same moment Musō found himself without power to move or speak. He saw that Shape lift the corpse, as with hands, devour it, more quickly than a cat devours a rat – beginning at the head, and eating everything: the hair and the bones and even the shroud. And the monstrous Thing, having thus consumed the body, turned to the offerings, and ate them also. Then it went away, as mysteriously as it had come.

When the villagers returned next morning, they found the priest awaiting them at the door of the headman's dwelling. All in turn saluted him; and when they had entered, and looked about the room, no one expressed any surprise at the disappearance of the dead body and the offerings. But the master of the house said to Musō:

'Reverend Sir, you have probably seen unpleasant things during the night: all of us were anxious about you. But now we are very happy to find you alive and unharmed. Gladly we would have stayed with you, if it had been possible. But the law of our village, as I told you last evening, obliges us to quit our houses after a death has taken place, and to leave the corpse alone. Whenever this law has been broken, heretofore, some great misfortune has followed. Whenever it is obeyed, we find that the corpse and the offerings disappear during our absence. Perhaps you have seen the cause.'

Then Musō told of the dim and awful Shape that had entered the death-chamber to devour the body and the offerings. No person seemed to be surprised by his narration; and the master of the house observed:

'What you have told us, reverend Sir, agrees with what has been said about this matter from ancient time.'

Musō then inquired:

'Does not the priest on the hill sometimes perform the funeral service for your dead?'

'What priest?' the young man asked.

'The priest who yesterday evening directed me to this village,' answered Musō. 'I called at his *anjitsu* on the hill yonder. He refused me lodging, but told me the way here.'

The listeners looked at each other, as in astonishment; and, after a moment of silence, the master of the house said:

'Reverend Sir, there is no priest and there is no *anjitsu* on the hill. For the time of many generations there has not been any resident-priest in this neighborhood.'

Musō said nothing more on the subject; for it was evident that his kind hosts supposed him to have been deluded by some goblin. But after having bidden them farewell, and obtained all necessary information as to his road, he determined to look again for the hermitage on the hill, and so to ascertain whether he had really been deceived. He found the *anjitsu* without any difficulty; and, this time, its aged occupant invited him to enter. When he had done so, the hermit humbly bowed down before him, exclaiming: 'Ah! I am ashamed! – I am very much ashamed! – I am exceedingly ashamed!'

'You need not be ashamed for having refused me shelter,' said Musō. 'You directed me to the village yonder, where I was very kindly treated; and I thank you for that favor.'

'I can give no man shelter,' the recluse made answer; 'and it is not for the refusal that I am ashamed. I am ashamed only that you should have seen me in my real shape – for it was I who devoured the corpse and the offerings last night before your eyes . . . Know, reverend Sir, that I am a *jikininki** – an eater of human flesh. Have pity upon me, and suffer me to confess the secret fault by which I became reduced to this condition.

'A long, long time ago, I was a priest in this desolate region. There was no other priest for many leagues around.

---

* Literally, a man-eating goblin. The Japanese narrator gives also the Sanscrit term, 'Râkshasa'; but this word is quite as vague as *jikininki*, since there are many kinds of Râkshasas. Apparently the word *jikininki* signifies here one of the *Baramon-Rasetsu-Gaki* – forming the twenty-sixth class of pretas enumerated in the old Buddhist books.

So, in that time, the bodies of the mountain-folk who died used to be brought here – sometimes from great distances – in order that I might repeat over them the holy service. But I repeated the service and performed the rites only as a matter of business; I thought only of the food and the clothes that my sacred profession enabled me to gain. And because of this selfish impiety I was reborn, immediately after my death, into the state of a *jikininki*. Since then I have been obliged to feed upon the corpses of the people who die in this district: every one of them I must devour in the way that you saw last night . . . Now, reverend Sir, let me beseech you to perform a *Ségaki*-service* for me: help me by your prayers, I entreat you, so that I may be soon able to escape from this horrible state of existence.' . . .

No sooner had the hermit uttered this petition than he disappeared; and the hermitage also disappeared at the same instant. And Musō Kokushi found himself kneeling alone in the high grass, beside an ancient and moss-grown tomb of the form called *go-rin-ishi*,† which seemed to be the tomb of a priest.

---

* A Ségaki-service is a special Buddhist service performed on behalf of beings supposed to have entered into the condition of *gaki* (pretas), or hungry spirits. For a brief account of such a service, see my *Japanese Miscellany*.

† Literally, 'five- circle [or "five- zone"] stone'. A funeral monument consisting of five parts superimposed – each a different form – symbolizing the five mystic elements: Ether, Air, Fire, Water, Earth.

Mujina

On the Akasaka Road, in Tōkyō, there is a slope called Kii-no-kuni-zaka – which means the Slope of the Province of Kii. I do not know why it is called the Slope of the Province of Kii. On one side of this slope you see an ancient moat, deep and very wide, with high green banks rising up to some place of gardens; and on the other side of the road extend the long and lofty walls of an imperial palace. Before the era of street-lamps and *jinrikishas*, this neighborhood was very lonesome after dark; and belated pedestrians would go miles out of their way rather than mount the Kii-no-kuni-zaka, alone, after sunset.

All because of a Mujina that used to walk there.

The last man who saw the Mujina was an old merchant of the Kyōbashi quarter, who died about thirty years ago. This is the story, as he told it:

One night, at a late hour, he was hurrying up the Kii-no-kuni-zaka, when he perceived a woman crouching by the moat, all alone, and weeping bitterly. Fearing that she intended to drown herself, he stopped to offer her any assistance or consolation in his power. She appeared to be a slight and graceful person, handsomely dressed; and her hair was arranged like that of a young girl of good family. 'O-jochū,'* he exclaimed, approaching her – 'O-jochū, do not cry like that! . . . Tell me what the trouble is; and if there be any way to help you, I shall be glad to help you.' (He really meant what he said; for he was a very kind man.) But she continued to weep – hiding her face from him with one of her long sleeves. 'O-jochū,' he said again, as gently as he could – 'please, please listen to me! . . . This is no place for a young lady at night! Do not cry, I implore you! – only tell me how I may be of some help to you!' Slowly she rose up, but turned her back to him, and continued to moan and sob behind her sleeve. He laid his hand lightly upon her shoulder, and pleaded: 'O-jochū! – O-jochū! – O-jochū! . . . Listen to me, just for one little moment! . . . O-jochū! – O-jochū!' . . . Then that O-jochū turned around, and dropped her sleeve, and stroked her face with her hand; and the man saw that she had no eyes or nose or mouth – and he screamed and ran away.

Up Kii-no-kuni-zaka he ran and ran; and all was black and empty before him. On and on he ran, never daring to look back; and at last he saw a lantern, so far away that it looked like the gleam of a firefly; and he made for it. It proved to be only the lantern of an itinerant *soba*-seller,†

---

* O-jochū ('honourable damsel') – a polite form of address used in speaking to a young lady whom one does not know.
† Soba is a preparation of buckwheat, somewhat resembling vermicelli.

who had set down his stand by the road-side; but any light and any human companionship was good after that experience; and he flung himself down at the feet of the *soba*-seller, crying out, 'Ah! – aa!! – *aa!!!*' . . .

'*Koré! Koré!*' roughly exclaimed the *soba*-man. 'Here! what is the matter with you? Anybody hurt you?'

'No – nobody hurt me,' panted the other – 'only . . . *Ah! – aa!*' . . .

'– Only scared you?' queried the peddler, unsympathetically. 'Robbers?'

'Not robbers – not robbers,' gasped the terrified man . . . 'I saw . . . I saw a woman – by the moat; and she showed me . . . *Ah!* I cannot tell you what she showed me!' . . .

'*Hé!* Was it anything like THIS that she showed you?' cried the *soba*-man, stroking his own face – which therewith became like unto an Egg . . . And, simultaneously, the light went out.

Rokuro-Kubi

Nearly five hundred years ago there was a samurai, named Isogai Héïdazaëmon Takétsura, in the service of the Lord Kikuji, of Kyūshū. This Isogai had inherited, from many warlike ancestors, a natural aptitude for military exercises, and extraordinary strength. While yet a boy he had surpassed his teachers in the art of swordsmanship, in archery, and in the use of the spear, and had displayed all the capacities of a daring and skillful soldier. Afterwards, in the time of the Eikyō* war, he so distinguished himself that high honors were bestowed upon him. But when the house of Kikuji came to ruin, Isogai found himself without a master. He might then easily have obtained service under another *daimyō*; but as he had never sought distinction for his own sake alone, and as his heart remained true to his former lord, he preferred to give up the world. So he cut off his hair, and became a traveling priest – taking the Buddhist name of Kwairyō.

But always, under the *koromo*† of the priest, Kwairyō

---

* The period of Eikyō lasted from 1429 to 1441.
† The upper robe of a Buddhist priest is thus called.

kept warm within him the heart of the samurai. As in other years he had laughed at peril, so now also he scorned danger; and in all weathers and all seasons he journeyed to preach the good Law in places where no other priest would have dared to go. For that age was an age of violence and disorder; and upon the highways there was no security for the solitary traveler, even if he happened to be a priest.

In the course of his first long journey, Kwairyō had occasion to visit the province of Kai. One evening, as he was traveling through the mountains of that province, darkness overcame him in a very lonesome district, leagues away from any village. So he resigned himself to pass the night under the stars; and having found a suitable grassy spot, by the roadside, he lay down there, and prepared to sleep. He had always welcomed discomfort; and even a bare rock was for him a good bed, when nothing better could be found, and the root of a pine-tree an excellent pillow. His body was iron; and he never troubled himself about dews or rain or frost or snow.

Scarcely had he lain down when a man came along the road, carrying an axe and a great bundle of chopped wood. This woodcutter halted on seeing Kwairyō lying down, and, after a moment of silent observation, said to him in a tone of great surprise:

'What kind of a man can you be, good Sir, that you dare to lie down alone in such a place as this? . . . There are haunters about here – many of them. Are you not afraid of Hairy Things?'

'My friend,' cheerfully answered Kwairyō, 'I am only a wandering priest – a "Cloud-and-Water-Guest", as folks call it: *Unsui-no-ryokaku*. And I am not in the least afraid of Hairy Things – if you mean goblin-foxes, or goblin-badgers, or any creatures of that kind. As for lonesome places, I like them: they are suitable for meditation. I am accustomed to sleeping in the open air: and I have learned never to be anxious about my life.'

'You must be indeed a brave man, Sir Priest,' the peasant responded, 'to lie down here! This place has a bad name – a very bad name. But, as the proverb has it, *Kunshi ayayuki ni chikayorazu* ['The superior man does not needlessly expose himself to peril']; and I must assure you, Sir, that it is very dangerous to sleep here. Therefore, although my house is only a wretched thatched hut, let me beg of you to come home with me at once. In the way of food, I have nothing to offer you; but there is a roof at least, and you can sleep under it without risk.'

He spoke earnestly; and Kwairyō, liking the kindly tone of the man, accepted this modest offer. The woodcutter guided him along a narrow path, leading up from the main road through mountain-forest. It was a rough and dangerous path – sometimes skirting precipices – sometimes offering nothing but a network of slippery roots for the foot to rest upon – sometimes winding over or between masses of jagged rock. But at last Kwairyō found himself upon a cleared space at the top of a hill, with a full moon shining overhead; and he saw before him a small thatched cottage, cheerfully lighted from within. The woodcutter led him to a shed at the back of the house, whither water had been conducted, through bamboo-pipes, from some neighboring stream; and the two men washed their feet. Beyond the shed was a vegetable garden, and a grove of cedars and bamboos; and beyond the trees appeared the glimmer of a cascade, pouring from some loftier height, and swaying in the moonshine like a long white robe.

As Kwairyō entered the cottage with his guide, he perceived four persons – men and women – warming their hands at a little fire kindled in the *ro** of the principal apartment. They bowed low to the priest, and greeted him in the most respectful manner. Kwairyō wondered that persons so poor, and dwelling in such a solitude, should be aware of the polite forms of greeting. 'These are good people,' he thought to himself; 'and they must have been taught by some one well acquainted with the rules of propriety.' Then turning to his host – the *aruji*, or house-master, as the others called him – Kwairyō said:

'From the kindness of your speech, and from the very

---

* A sort of little fireplace, contrived in the floor of a room, is thus described. The *ro* is usually a square shallow cavity, lined with metal and half-filled with ashes, in which charcoal is lighted.

polite welcome given me by your household, I imagine
that you have not always been a woodcutter. Perhaps you
formerly belonged to one of the upper classes?'

Smiling, the woodcutter answered:

'Sir, you are not mistaken. Though now living as you
find me, I was once a person of some distinction. My story
is the story of a ruined life – ruined by my own fault. I
used to be in the service of a *daimyō*; and my rank in that
service was not inconsiderable. But I loved women and
wine too well; and under the influence of passion I acted
wickedly. My selfishness brought about the ruin of our
house, and caused the death of many persons. Retribu-
tion followed me; and I long remained a fugitive in the
land. Now I often pray that I may be able to make some
atonement for the evil which I did, and to reestablish the
ancestral home. But I fear that I shall never find any way
of so doing. Nevertheless, I try to overcome the karma of
my errors by sincere repentance, and by helping as afar
as I can, those who are unfortunate.'

Kwairyō was pleased by this announcement of good
resolve; and he said to the *aruji*:

'My friend, I have had occasion to observe that man,
prone to folly in their youth, may in after years become
very earnest in right living. In the holy sûtras it is written
that those strongest in wrong-doing can become, by
power of good resolve, the strongest in right-doing. I do
not doubt that you have a good heart; and I hope that
better fortune will come to you. To-night I shall recite

the sûtras for your sake, and pray that you may obtain the force to overcome the karma of any past errors.'

With these assurances, Kwairyō bade the *aruji* good-night; and his host showed him to a very small side-room, where a bed had been made ready. Then all went to sleep except the priest, who began to read the sûtras by the light of a paper lantern. Until a late hour he continued to read and pray: then he opened a little window in his little sleeping-room, to take a last look at the landscape before lying down. The night was beautiful: there was no cloud in the sky: there was no wind; and the strong moon-light threw down sharp black shadows of foliage, and glittered on the dews of the garden. Shrillings of crickets and bell-insects made a musical tumult; and the sound of the neighboring cascade deepened with the night. Kwairyō felt thirsty as he listened to the noise of the water; and, remembering the bamboo aqueduct at the rear of the house, he thought that he could go there and get a drink without disturbing the sleeping household. Very gently he pushed apart the sliding-screens that separated his room from the main apartment; and he saw, by the light of the lantern, five recumbent bodies – without heads!

For one instant he stood bewildered – imagining a crime. But in another moment he perceived that there was no blood, and that the headless necks did not look as if they had been cut. Then he thought to himself: 'Either this is an illusion made by goblins, or I have been lured into the dwelling of a Rokuro-Kubi . . . In the book *Sōshinki* it is written that if one find the body of a Rokuro-Kubi without its head, and remove the body to another place, the head will never be able to join itself again to the neck. And the book further says that when the head comes back and finds that its body has been moved, it will strike itself upon the floor three times – bounding like a ball – and will pant as in great fear, and presently die. Now, if these be Rokuro-Kubi, they mean me no good; so I shall be justified in following the instructions of the book.' . . .

He seized the body of the *aruji* by the feet, pulled it to the window, and pushed it out. Then he went to the back-door, which he found barred; and he surmised that the heads had made their exit through the smoke-hole in the roof, which had been left open. Gently unbarring the door, he made his way to the garden, and proceeded with all possible caution to the grove beyond it. He heard voices talking in the grove; and he went in the direction of the voices – stealing from shadow to shadow, until he reached a good hiding-place. Then, from behind a trunk, he caught sight of the heads – all five of them – flitting about, and chatting as they flitted. They were eating worms and insects which they found on the ground or among the trees. Presently the head of the *aruji* stopped eating and said:

'Ah, that traveling priest who came to-night! – how fat all his body is! When we shall have eaten him, our bellies will be well filled . . . I was foolish to talk to him as I did; it only set him to reciting the sûtras on behalf of my soul! To go near him while he is reciting would be difficult; and we cannot touch him so long as he is praying. But as it is now nearly morning, perhaps he has gone to sleep . . . Some one of you go to the house and see what the fellow is doing.'

Another head – the head of a young woman – immediately rose up and flitted to the house, lightly as a bat. After a few minutes it came back, and cried out huskily, in a tone of great alarm: 'That traveling priest is not in the house; he is gone! But that is not the worst of the matter. He has taken the body of our *aruji*; and I do not know where he has put it.'

At this announcement the head of the *aruji* – distinctly visible in the moonlight – assumed a frightful aspect: its eyes opened monstrously; its hair stood up bristling; and its teeth gnashed. Then a cry burst from its lips; and – weeping tears of rage – it exclaimed:

'Since my body has been moved, to rejoin it is not possible! Then I must die! . . . And all through the work of that priest! Before I die I will get at that priest! – I will tear him! – I will devour him! . . . *And there he is* – behind that tree! – hiding behind that tree! See him! – the fat coward!' . . . In the same moment the head of the *aruji*, followed by the other four heads, sprang at Kwairyō. But the strong priest had already armed himself by plucking up a young tree; and with that tree he struck the heads as they came – knocking them from him with tremendous blows. Four of them fled away. But the head of the *aruji*, though battered again and again, desperately continued to bound at the priest, and at last caught him by the left sleeve of his robe. Kwairyō, however, as quickly gripped the head by its topknot, and repeatedly struck it. It did not release its hold; but it uttered a long moan, and thereafter ceased to struggle. It was dead. But its teeth still held the sleeve; and, for all his great strength, Kwairyō could not force open the jaws.

With the head still hanging to his sleeve he went back to the house, and there caught sight of the other four Rokuro-Kubi squatting together, with their bruised and bleeding heads reunited to their bodies. But when they perceived him at the back-door all screamed, 'The priest! the priest!' – and fled, through the other doorway, out into the woods.

Eastward the sky was brightening; day was about to dawn; and Kwairyō knew that the power of the goblins was limited to the hours of darkness. He looked at the head clinging to his sleeve – its face all fouled with blood and foam and clay; and he laughed aloud as he thought to himself: 'What a *miyagé*!* – the head of a goblin!' After

---

* A present made to friends or to the household on returning from a journey is thus called. Ordinarily, of course, the miyagé consists of something produced in the locality to which the journey has been made: this is the point of Kwairyō's jest.

which he gathered together his few belongings, and leisurely descended the mountain to continue his journey.

Right on he journeyed, until he came to Suwa in Shinano; and into the main street of Suwa he solemnly strode, with the head dangling at his elbow. Then woman fainted, and children screamed and ran away; and there was a great crowding and clamoring until the *torité* (as the police in those days were called) seized the priest, and took him to jail. For they supposed the head to be the head of a murdered man who, in the moment of being killed, had caught the murderer's sleeve in his teeth. As for the Kwairyō, he only smiled and said nothing when they questioned him. So, after having passed a night in prison, he was brought before the magistrates of the district. Then he was ordered to explain how he, a priest, had been found with the head of a man fastened to his sleeve, and why he had dared thus shamelessly to parade his crime in the sight of people.

Kwairyō laughed long and loudly at these questions; and then he said:

'Sirs, I did not fasten the head to my sleeve: it fastened itself there – much against my will. And I have not committed any crime. For this is not the head of a man; it is the head of a goblin; and, if I caused the death of the goblin, I did not do so by any shedding of blood, but simply by taking the precautions necessary to assure my own safety.' . . . And he proceeded to relate the whole of the adventure – bursting into another hearty laugh as he told of his encounter with the five heads. But the magistrates did not laugh. They judged him to be a hardened criminal, and his story an insult to their intelligence. Therefore, without further questioning, they decided to order his immediate execution – all of them except one, a very old man. This aged officer had made no remark during the trial; but, after having heard the opinion of his colleagues, he rose up, and said: 'Let us first examine the head carefully; for this, I think, has not yet been done. If the priest has spoken truth, the head itself should bear witness for him . . . Bring the head here!'

So the head, still holding in its teeth the *koromo* that had been stripped from Kwairyō's shoulders, was put before the judges. The old man turned it round and round, carefully examined it, and discovered, on the nape of its neck, several strange red characters. He called the attention of his colleagues to these, and also bade them observe that the edges of the neck nowhere presented the appearance of having been cut by any weapon. On the contrary, the line of leverance was smooth as the line at which a falling leaf detaches itself from the stem . . . Then said the elder:

'I am quite sure that the priest told us nothing but the truth. This is the head of a Rokuro-Kubi. In the book *Nan-hō-ï-butsu-shi* it is written that certain red characters can always be found upon the nape of the neck of a real Rokuro-Kubi. There are the characters: you can see for yourselves that they have not been painted.

Moreover, it is well known that such goblins have been dwelling in the mountains of the province of Kai from very ancient time . . . But you, Sir,' he exclaimed, turning to Kwairyō – 'what sort of sturdy priest may you be? Certainly you have given proof of a courage that few priests possess; and you have the air of a soldier rather than a priest. Perhaps you once belonged to the samurai-class?'

'You have guessed rightly, Sir,' Kwairyō responded. 'Before becoming a priest, I long followed the profession of arms; and in those days I never feared man or devil. My name then was Isogai Héïdazaëmon Takétsura of Kyūshū: there may be some among you who remember it.'

At the mention of that name, a murmur of admiration filled the court-room; for there were many present who remembered it. And Kwairyō immediately found himself among friends instead of judges – friends anxious to prove their admiration by fraternal kindness. With honor they escorted him to the residence of the *daimyō*, who welcomed him, and feasted him, and made him a handsome present before allowing him to depart. When Kwairyō left Suwa, he was as happy as any priest is permitted to be in this transitory world. As for the head, he took it with him – jocosely insisting that he intended it for a *miyagé*.

And now it only remains to tell what became of the head.

*

A day or two after leaving Suwa, Kwairyō met with a robber, who stopped him in a lonesome place, and bade him strip. Kwairyō at once removed his *koromo*, and offered it to the robber, who then first perceived what was hanging to the sleeve. Though brave, the highwayman was startled: he dropped the garment, and sprang back. Then he cried out: 'You! – what kind of a priest are you? Why, you are a worse man than I am! It is true that I have killed people; but I never walked about with anybody's head fastened to my sleeve . . . Well, Sir priest, I suppose we are of the same calling; and I must say that I admire you! . . . Now that head would be of use to me: I could frighten people with it. Will you sell it? You can have my robe in exchange for your *koromo*; and I will give you five *ryō* for the head.'

Kwairyō answered:

'I shall let you have the head and the robe if you insist; but I must tell you that this is not the head of a man. It is a goblin's head. So, if you buy it, and have any trouble in consequence, please to remember that you were not deceived by me.'

'What a nice priest you are!' exclaimed the robber. 'You kill men, and jest about it! . . . But I am really in earnest. Here is my robe; and here is the money; and let me have the head . . . What is the use of joking?'

'Take the thing,' said Kwairyō. 'I was not joking. The only joke – if there be any joke at all – is that you are fool enough to pay good money for a goblin's head.' And Kwairyō, loudly laughing, went upon his way.

Thus the robber got the head and the *koromo*; and for some time he played goblin-priest upon the highways. But, reaching the neighborhood of Suwa, he there learned the true story of the head; and he then became afraid that the spirit of the Rokuro-Kubi might give him trouble. So he made up his mind to take back the head to the place from which it had come, and to bury it with its body. He found his way to the lonely cottage in the mountains of Kai; but nobody was there, and he could not discover the body. Therefore he buried the head by itself, in the grove behind the cottage; and he had a tombstone set up over the grave; and he caused a *Ségaki*-service to be performed on behalf of the spirit of the Rokuro-Kubi. And that tombstone – known as the Tombstone of the Rokuro-Kubi – may be seen (at least so the Japanese story-teller declares) even unto this day.

The Story of Aoyagi

In the era of Bummei [1469–1486] there was a young samurai called Tomotada in the service of Hatakéyama
Yoshimuné, the Lord of Noto. Tomotada was a native of
Echizen; but at an early age he had been taken, as page,
into the palace of the *daimyō* of Noto, and had been edu-
cated, under the supervision of that prince, for the
profession of arms. As he grew up, he proved himself both
a good scholar and a good soldier, and continued to enjoy
the favor of his prince. Being gifted with an amiable character, a winning address, and a very handsome person, he
was admired and much liked by his samurai-comrades.

When Tomotada was about twenty years old, he was
sent upon a private mission to Hosokawa Masamoto, the
great *daimyō* of Kyōto, a kinsman of Hatakéyama Yoshimuné. Having been ordered to journey through Echizen,
the youth requested and obtained permission to pay a
visit, on the way, to his widowed mother.

It was the coldest period of the year when he started;
and, though mounted upon a powerful horse, he found
himself obliged to proceed slowly. The road which he
followed passed through a mountain-district where the

settlements were few and far between; and on the second day of his journey, after a weary ride of hours, he was dismayed to find that he could not reach his intended halting-place until late in the night. He had reason to be anxious; for a heavy snowstorm came on, with an intensely cold wind; and the horse showed signs of exhaustion. But in that trying moment, Tomotada unexpectedly perceived the thatched roof of a cottage on the summit of a near hill, where willow-trees were growing. With difficulty he urged his tired animal to the dwelling; and he loudly knocked upon the storm-doors, which had been closed against the wind. An old woman opened them, and cried out compassionately at the sight of the handsome stranger: 'Ah, how pitiful! – a young gentleman traveling alone in such weather! . . . Deign, young master, to enter.'

Tomotada dismounted, and after leading his horse to a shed in the rear, entered the cottage, where he saw an old man and a girl warming themselves by a fire of bamboo splints. They respectfully invited him to approach the fire; and the old folks then proceeded to warm some rice-wine, and to prepare food for the traveler, whom they ventured to question in regard to his journey. Meanwhile the young girl disappeared behind a screen. Tomotada had observed, with astonishment, that she was extremely beautiful – though her attire was of the most wretched kind, and her long, loose hair in disorder. He wondered that so handsome a girl should be living in such a miserable and lonesome place.

The old man said to him:

'Honored Sir, the next village is far; and the snow is falling thickly. The wind is piercing; and the road is very bad. Therefore, to proceed further this night would probably be dangerous. Although this hovel is unworthy of your presence, and although we have not any comfort to offer, perhaps it were safer to remain to-night under this miserable roof ... We would take good care of your horse.'

Tomotada accepted this humble proposal – secretly glad of the chance thus afforded him to see more of the young girl. Presently a coarse but ample meal was set before him; and the girl came from behind the screen, to serve the wine. She was now reclad, in a rough but cleanly robe of homespun; and her long, loose hair had been neatly combed and smoothed. As she bent forward to fill his cup, Tomotada was amazed to perceive that she was incomparably more beautiful than any woman whom he had ever before seen; and there was a grace about her every motion that astonished him. But the elders began to apologize for her, saying: 'Sir, our daughter, Aoyagi,* has been brought up here in the mountains, almost alone; and she knows nothing of gentle service. We pray that you will pardon her stupidity and her ignorance.' Tomotada protested that he deemed himself lucky to be waited

* The name signifies 'Green Willow'; though rarely met with, it is still in use.

upon by so comely a maiden. He could not turn his eyes
away from her – though he saw that his admiring gaze
made her blush; and he left the wine and food untasted
before him. The mother said: 'Kind Sir, we very much
hope that you will try to eat and to drink a little – though
our peasant-fare is of the worst – as you must have been
chilled by that piercing wind.' Then, to please the old
folks, Tomotada ate and drank as he could; but the charm
of the blushing girl still grew upon him. He talked with
her, and found that her speech was sweet as her face.
Brought up in the mountains as she might have been;
but, in that case, her parents must at some time have been
persons of high degree; for she spoke and moved like a
damsel of rank. Suddenly he addressed her with a poem –
which was also a question – inspired by the delight in his
heart:

> *'Tadzunétsuru,*
> *Hana ka toté koso,*
> *Hi wo kurasé,*
> *Akénu ni otoru*
> *Akané sasuran?'*

['*Being on my way to pay a visit, I found that which I took to be a
flower: therefore here I spend the day . . . Why, in the time before dawn,
the dawn-blush tint should glow – that, indeed, I know not.*']*

---

* The poem may be read in two ways; several of the phrases having a
double meaning. But the art of its construction would need considerable

Without a moment's hesitation, she answered him in these verses:

> *'Izuru hi no*
> *Honoméku iro wo*
> *Waga sodé ni*
> *Tsutsumaba asu mo*
> *Kimiya tomaran.'*

[*'If with my sleeve I hid the faint fair color of the dawning sun – then, perhaps, in the morning my lord will remain.'*]*

Then Tomotada knew that she accepted his admiration; and he was scarcely less surprised by the art with which she had uttered her feelings in verse, than delighted by the assurance which the verses conveyed. He was now certain that in all this world he could not hope to meet, much less to win, a girl more beautiful and witty than this rustic maid before him; and a voice in his heart seemed to cry out urgently, 'Take the luck that the gods have put in your way!' In short he was bewitched – bewitched to such a degree that, without further

---

space to explain, and could scarcely interest the Western reader. The meaning which Tomotada desired to convey might be thus expressed: 'While journeying to visit my mother, I met with a being lovely as a flower; and for the sake of that lovely person, I am passing the day here . . . Fair one, wherefore that dawnlike blush before the hour of dawn? – can it mean that you love me?'

* Another reading is possible; but this one gives the significance of the answer intended.

preliminary, he asked the old people to give him their daughter in marriage – telling them, at the same time, his name and lineage, and his rank in the train of the Lord of Noto.

They bowed down before him, with many exclamations of grateful astonishment. But, after some moments of apparent hesitation, the father replied:

'Honored master, you are a person of high position, and likely to rise to still higher things. Too great is the favor that you deign to offer us; indeed, the depth of our gratitude therefore is not to be spoken or measured. But this girl of ours, being a stupid country-girl of vulgar birth, with no training or teaching of any sort, it would be improper to let her become the wife of a noble samurai. Even to speak of such a matter is not right . . . But, since you find the girl to your liking, and have condescended to pardon her peasant-manners and to overlook her great rudeness, we do gladly present her to you, for a humble handmaid. Deign, therefore, to act hereafter in her regard according to your august pleasure.'

Ere morning the storm had passed; and day broke through a cloudless east. Even if the sleeve of Aoyagi hid from her lover's eyes the rose-blush of that dawn, he could no longer tarry. But neither could he resign himself to part with the girl; and, when everything had been prepared for his journey, he thus addressed her parents:

'Though it may seem thankless to ask for more than I have already received, I must again beg you to give me

175

your daughter for wife. It would be difficult for me to separate from her now; and as she is willing to accompany me, if you permit, I can take her with me as she is. If you will give her to me, I shall ever cherish you as parents . . . And, in the meantime, please to accept this poor acknowledgment of your kindest hospitality.'

So saying, he placed before his humble host a purse of gold *ryō*. But the old man, after many prostrations, gently pushed back the gift, and said:

'Kind master, the gold would be of no use to us; and you will probably have need of it during your long, cold journey. Here we buy nothing; and we could not spend so much money upon ourselves, even if we wished . . . As for the girl, we have already bestowed her as a free gift; she belongs to you: therefore it is not necessary to ask our leave to take her away. Already she has told us that she hopes to accompany you, and to remain your servant for as long as you may be willing to endure her presence. We are only too happy to know that you deign to accept her; and we pray that you will not trouble yourself on our account. In this place we could not provide her with proper clothing – much less with a dowry. Moreover, being old, we should in any event have to separate from her before long. Therefore it is very fortunate that you should be willing to take her with you now.'

It was in vain that Tomotada tried to persuade the old people to accept a present: he found that they cared nothing for money. But he saw that they were really anxious to trust their daughter's fate to his hands; and he therefore decided to take her with him. So he placed her upon his horse, and bade the old folks farewell for the time being, with many sincere expressions of gratitude. 'Honored Sir,' the father made answer, 'it is we, and not you, who have reason for gratitude. We are sure that you will be kind to our girl; and we have no fears for her sake.' . . .

[*Here, in the Japanese original, there is a queer break in the natural course of the narration, which therefrom remains curiously inconsistent. Nothing further is said about the mother of Tomotada, or about the parents of Aoyagi, or about the* daimyō *of Noto. Evidently the writer wearied of his work at this point, and hurried the story, very carelessly, to its startling end. I am not able to supply his omissions, or to repair his faults of construction; but I must venture to put in a few explanatory details, without which the rest of the tale would not hold together . . . It appears that Tomotada rashly took Aoyagi with him to Kyōto, and so got into trouble; but we are not informed as to where the couple lived afterwards.*]

. . . Now a samurai was not allowed to marry without the consent of his lord; and Tomotada could not expect to obtain this sanction before his mission had been accomplished. He had reason, under such circumstances, to fear that the beauty of Aoyagi might attract dangerous attention, and that means might be devised of taking her away from him. In Kyōto he therefore tried to keep her hidden from curious eyes. But a retainer of Lord Hosokawa one day caught sight of Aoyagi, discovered her relation to Tomotada, and reported the matter to the *daimyō*. Thereupon the *daimyō* – a young prince, and fond of pretty faces – gave orders that the girl should be brought to the palace; and she was taken thither at once, without ceremony.

Tomotada sorrowed unspeakably; but he knew himself powerless. He was only an humble messenger in the service of a far-off *daimyō*; and for the time being he was at the mercy of a much more powerful *daimyō*, whose wishes were not to be questioned. Moreover Tomotada knew that he had acted foolishly – that he had brought about his own misfortune, by entering into a clandestine relation which the code of the military class condemned. There was now but one hope for him – a desperate hope: that Aoyagi might be able and willing to escape and to flee with him. After long reflection, he resolved to try to send her a letter. The attempt would be dangerous, of course: any writing sent to her might find its way to the hands of the *daimyō*; and to send a love-letter to any inmate of the palace was an unpardonable offense. But he resolved to dare the risk; and, in the form of a Chinese poem, he composed a letter which he endeavored to have conveyed to her. The poem was written with only twenty-eight characters. But with those twenty-eight characters he was about to express all the depth of his passion, and to suggest all the pain of his loss:*

> *Kōshi ō-son gojin wo ou;*
> *Ryokuju namida wo tarété rakin wo hitataru;*
> *Komon hitotabi irité fukaki koto umi no gotoshi;*
> *Koré yori shorō koré rojin*

[*Closely, closely the youthful prince now follows after the gem-bright maid;*
The tears of the fair one, falling, have moistened all her robes.
But the august lord, having once become enamored of her – the depth of his longing is like the depth of the sea.
Therefore it is only I that am left forlorn – only I that am left to wander along.]

On the evening of the day after this poem had been sent, Tomotada was summoned to appear before the Lord Hosokawa. The youth at once suspected that his confidence had been betrayed; and he could not hope, if his letter had been seen by the *daimyō*, to escape the severest penalty. 'Now he will order my death,' thought Tomotada; 'but I do not care to live unless Aoyagi be restored to me.

---

* So the Japanese story-teller would have us believe – although the verses seem commonplace in translation. I have tried to give only their general meaning: an effective literal translation would require some scholarship.

Besides, if the death-sentence be passed, I can at least try to kill Hosokawa.' He slipped his swords into his girdle, and hastened to the palace.

On entering the presence-room he saw the Lord Hosokawa seated upon the dais, surrounded by samurai of high rank, in caps and robes of ceremony. All were silent as statues; and while Tomotada advanced to make obeisance, the hush seemed to him sinister and heavy, like the stillness before a storm. But Hosokawa suddenly descended from the dais, and, while taking the youth by the arm, began to repeat the words of the poem: '*Kōshi ō-son gojin wo ou.*' . . . And Tomotada, looking up, saw kindly tears in the prince's eyes.

Then said Hosokawa:

'Because you love each other so much, I have taken it upon myself to authorize your marriage, in lieu of my kinsman, the Lord of Noto; and your wedding shall now be celebrated before me. The guests are assembled; the gifts are ready.'

At a signal from the lord, the sliding-screens concealing a further apartment were pushed open; and Tomotada saw there many dignitaries of the court, assembled for the ceremony, and Aoyagi awaiting him in bride's apparel . . . Thus was she given back to him; and the wedding was joyous and splendid; and precious gifts were made to the young couple by the prince, and by the members of his household.

*

For five happy years, after that wedding, Tomotada and Aoyagi dwelt together. But one morning Aoyagi, while talking with her husband about some household matter, suddenly uttered a great cry of pain, and then became very white and still. After a few moments she said, in a feeble voice: 'Pardon me for thus rudely crying out – but the pain was so sudden! . . . My dear husband, our union must have been brought about through some karma-relation in a former state of existence; and that happy relation, I think, will bring us again together in more than one life to come. But for this present existence of ours, the relation is now ended; – we are about to be separated. Repeat for me, I beseech you, the *Nembutsu*-prayer – because I am dying.'

'Oh! what strange wild fancies!' cried the startled husband – 'you are only a little unwell, my dear one! . . . lie down for a while, and rest; and the sickness will pass.' . . .

'No, no!' she responded – 'I am dying! – I do not imagine it; I know! . . . And it were needless now, my dear husband, to hide the truth from you any longer: I am not a human being. The soul of a tree is my soul; the heart of a tree is my heart; the sap of the willow is my life. And some one, at this cruel moment, is cutting down my tree; that is why I must die! . . . Even to weep were now beyond my strength! – quickly, quickly repeat the *Nembutsu* for me . . . quickly! . . . Ah!' . . .

With another cry of pain she turned aside her beautiful head, and tried to hide her face behind her sleeve. But almost in the same moment her whole form appeared to collapse in the strangest way, and to sink down, down, down – level with the floor. Tomotada had spring to support her; but there was nothing to support! There lay on the matting only the empty robes of the fair creature and the ornaments that she had worn in her hair: the body had ceased to exist . . .

Tomotada shaved his head, took the Buddhist vows, and became an itinerant priest. He traveled through all the provinces of the empire; and, at holy places which he visited, he offered up prayers for the soul of Aoyagi. Reaching Echizen, in the course of his pilgrimage, he sought the home of the parents of his beloved. But when he arrived at the lonely place among the hills, where their dwelling had been, he found that the cottage had disappeared. There was nothing to mark even the spot where it had stood, except the stumps of three willows – two old trees and one young tree – that had been cut down long before his arrival.

Beside the stumps of those willow-trees he erected a memorial tomb, inscribed with divers holy texts; and he there performed many Buddhist services on behalf of the spirits of Aoyagi and of her parents.

The Story of Itō Norisuké

In the town of Uji, in the province of Yamashiro, there lived, about six hundred years ago, a young samurai named Itō Tatéwaki Norisuké, whose ancestors were of the Heiké clan. Itō was of handsome person and amiable character, a good scholar and apt at arms. But his family were poor; and he had no patron among the military nobility – so that his prospects were small. He lived in a very quiet way, devoting himself to the study of literature, and having (says the Japanese story-teller) 'only the Moon and the Wind for friends'.

One autumn evening, as he was taking a solitary walk in the neighborhood of the hill called Kotobikiyama, he happened to overtake a young girl who was following the same path. She was richly dressed, and seemed to be about eleven or twelve years old. Itō greeted her, and said, 'The sun will soon be setting, damsel, and this is rather a lonesome place. May I ask if you have lost your way?' She looked up at him with a bright smile, and answered deprecatingly: 'Nay! I am a *miya-dzukai*,* serving in this neighborhood; and I have only a little way to go.'

* August-residence servant.

By her use of the term *miya-dzukai*, Itō knew that the girl must be in the service of persons of rank; and her statement surprised him, because he had never heard of any family of distinction residing in that vicinity. But he only said: 'I am returning to Uji, where my home is. Perhaps you will allow me to accompany you on the way, as this is a very lonesome place.' She thanked him gracefully, seeming pleased by his offer; and they walked on together, chatting as they went. She talked about the weather, the flowers, the butterflies, and the birds; about a visit that she had once made to Uji, about the famous sights of the capital, where she had been born; and the moments passed pleasantly for Itō, as he listened to her fresh prattle. Presently, at a turn in the road, they entered a hamlet, densely shadowed by a grove of young trees.

[Here I must interrupt the story to tell you that, without having actually seen them, you cannot imagine how dark some Japanese country villages remain even in the brightest and hottest weather. In the neighborhood of Tōkyō itself there are many villages of this kind. At a short distance from such a settlement you see no houses: nothing is visible but a dense grove of evergreen trees. The grove, which is usually composed of young cedars and bamboos, serves to shelter the village from storms, and also to supply timber for various purposes. So closely are the trees planted that there is no room to pass between the trunks of them: they stand straight as masts, and mingle their crests so as to form a roof that excludes the sun. Each thatched cottage occupies a clear space in the plantation, the trees forming a fence about it, double the height of the building. Under the trees it is always twilight, even at high noon; and the houses, morning or evening, are half in shadow. What makes the first impression of such a village almost disquieting is, not the transparent gloom, which has a certain weird charm of its own, but the stillness. There may be fifty or a hundred dwellings; but you see nobody; and you hear no sound but the twitter of invisible birds, the occasional crowing of cocks, and the shrilling of cicadæ. Even the cicadæ, however, find these groves too dim, and sing faintly; being sun-lovers, they prefer the trees outside the village. I forgot to say that you may sometimes hear a viewless shuttle – *chaka-ton, chaka-ton*; but that familiar sound, in the great green silence, seems an elfish happening. The reason of the hush is simply that the people are not at home. All the adults, excepting some feeble elders, have gone to the neighboring fields, the women carrying their babies on their backs; and most of the children have gone to the nearest school, perhaps not less than a mile away. Verily, in these dim hushed villages, one seems to behold the mysterious perpetuation of conditions recorded in the texts of Kwang-Tze:

'*The ancients who had the nourishment of the world wished for nothing, and the world had enough: they did nothing, and*

*all things were transformed: their stillness was abysmal, and the
people were all composed.'*]

. . . The village was very dark when Itō reached it; for the
sun had set, and the after-glow made no twilight in the
shadowing of the trees. 'Now, kind sir,' the child said,
pointing to a narrow lane opening upon the main road,
'I have to go this way.' 'Permit me, then, to see you home,'
Itō responded; and he turned into the lane with her, feeling rather than seeing his way. But the girl soon stopped
before a small gate, dimly visible in the gloom – a gate
of trelliswork, beyond which the lights of a dwelling
could be seen. 'Here,' she said, 'is the honorable residence
in which I serve. As you have come thus far out of your
way, kind sir, will you not deign to enter and to rest a
while?' Itō assented. He was pleased by the informal invi-
tation; and he wished to learn what persons of superior
condition had chosen to reside in so lonesome a village.
He knew that sometimes a family of rank would retire in
this manner from public life, by reason of government
displeasure or political trouble; and he imagined that
such might be the history of the occupants of the dwelling
before him. Passing the gate, which his young guide
opened for him, he found himself in a large quaint garden. A miniature landscape, traversed by a winding
stream, was faintly distinguishable. 'Deign for one little
moment to wait,' the child said; 'I go to announce the
honorable coming;' and hurried toward the house. It

was a spacious house, but seemed very old, and built in the fashion of another time. The sliding-doors were not closed; but the lighted interior was concealed by a beautiful bamboo curtain extending along the gallery front. Behind it shadows were moving – shadows of women; and suddenly the music of a *koto* rippled into the night. So light and sweet was the playing that Itō could scarcely believe the evidence of his senses. A slumbrous feeling of delight stole over him as he listened – a delight strangely mingled with sadness. He wondered how any woman could have learned to play thus – wondered whether the player could be a woman – wondered even whether he was hearing earthly music; for enchantment seemed to have entered into his blood with the sound of it.

The soft music ceased; and almost at the same moment Itō found the little *miya-dzukai* beside him. 'Sir,' she said, 'it is requested that you will honorably enter.' She conducted him to the entrance, where he removed his sandals; and an aged woman, whom he thought to be the *Rōjo*, or matron of the household, came to welcome him at the threshold. The old woman then led him through many apartments to a large and well-lighted room in the rear of the house, and with many respectful salutations requested him to take the place of honor accorded to guests of distinction. He was surprised by the stateliness of the chamber, and the curious beauty of its decorations.

Presently some maid-servants brought refreshments; and he noticed that the cups and other vessels set before him were of rare and costly workmanship, and ornamented with a design indicating the high rank of the possessor. More and more he wondered what noble person had chosen this lonely retreat, and what happening could have inspired the wish for such solitude. But the aged attendant suddenly interrupted his reflections with the question:

'Am I wrong in supposing that you are Itō Sama, of Uji, Itō Tatéwaki Norisuké?'

Itō bowed in assent. He had not told his name to the little *miya-dzukai*, and the manner of the inquiry startled him.

'Please do not think my question rude,' continued the attendant. 'An old woman like myself may ask questions without improper curiosity. When you came to the house, I thought that I knew your face; and I asked your name only to clear away all doubt, before speaking of other matters. I have some thing of moment to tell you. You often pass through this village, and our young Himégimi-Sama* happened one morning to see you going by; and ever since that moment she has been thinking about you, day and night. Indeed, she thought so much that she became ill; and we have been very uneasy about her. For

---

* A scarcely translatable honorific title compounded of the word *himé* (princess) and *kimi* (sovereign, master or mistress, lord or lady, etc.).

that reason I took means to find out your name and residence; and I was on the point of sending you a letter
when – so unexpectedly! – you came to our gate with the
little attendant. Now, to say how happy I am to see you
is not possible; it seems almost too fortunate a happening
to be true! Really I think that this meeting must have
been brought about by the favor of Enmusubi-no-Kami –
that great God of Izumo who ties the knots of fortunate
union. And now that so lucky a destiny has led you hither,
perhaps you will not refuse – if there be no obstacle in
the way of such a union – to make happy the heart of our
Himégimi-Sama?'

For the moment Itō did not know how to reply. If the
old woman had spoken the truth, an extraordinary chance
was being offered to him. Only a great passion could
impel the daughter of a noble house to seek, of her own
will, the affection of an obscure and masterless samurai,
possessing neither wealth nor any sort of prospects. On
the other hand, it was not in the honorable nature of the
man to further his own interests by taking advantage of
a feminine weakness. Moreover, the circumstances were
disquietingly mysterious. Yet how to decline the proposal,
so unexpectedly made, troubled him not a little. After a
short silence, he replied:

'There would be no obstacle, as I have no wife, and
no betrothed, and no relation with any woman. Until now
I have lived with my parents; and the matter of my marriage was never discussed by them. You must know that

I am a poor samurai, without any patron among persons of rank; and I did not wish to marry until I could find some chance to improve my condition. As to the proposal which you have done me the very great honor to make, I can only say that I know myself yet unworthy of the notice of any noble maiden.'

The old woman smiled as if pleased by these words, and responded:

'Until you have seen our Himégimi-Sama, it were better that you make no decision. Perhaps you will feel no hesitation after you have seen her. Deign now to come with me, that I may present you to her.'

She conducted him to another larger guest-room, where preparations for a feast had been made, and having shown him the place of honor, left him for a moment alone. She returned accompanied by the Himégimi-Sama; and, at the first sight of the young mistress, Itō felt again the strange thrill of wonder and delight that had come to him in the garden, as he listened to the music of the *koto*. Never had he dreamed of so beautiful a being. Light seemed to radiate from her presence, and to shine through her garments, as the light of the moon through flossy clouds; her loosely flowing hair swayed about her as she moved, like the boughs of the drooping willow bestirred by the breezes of spring; her lips were like flowers of the peach besprinkled with morning dew. Itō was bewildered by the vision. He asked himself whether he was not looking upon the person of Amano-kawara-no-Ori-Himé herself, – the Weaving-Maiden who dwells by the shining River of Heaven.

Smiling, the aged woman turned to the fair one, who remained speechless, with downcast eyes and flushing cheeks, and said to her:

'See, my child! – at the moment when we could least have hoped for such a thing, the very person whom you wished to meet has come of his own accord. So fortunate a happening could have been brought about only by the will of the high gods. To think of it makes me weep for joy.' And she sobbed aloud. 'But now,' she continued, wiping away her tears with her sleeve, 'it only remains for you both – unless either prove unwilling, which I doubt – to pledge yourselves to each other, and to partake of your wedding feast.'

Itō answered by no word: the incomparable vision before him had numbed his will and tied his tongue. Maid-servants entered, bearing dishes and wine: the wedding feast was spread before the pair; and the pledges were given. Itō nevertheless remained as in a trance: the marvel of the adventure, and the wonder of the beauty of the bride, still bewildered him. A gladness, beyond aught that he had ever known before, filled his heart – like a great silence. But gradually he recovered his wonted calm; and thereafter he found himself able to converse without embarrassment. Of the wine he partook freely; and he ventured to speak, in a self-deprecating but merry way, about the doubts and fears that had oppressed him. Meanwhile the bride remained still as moonlight, never lifting her eyes, and replying only by a blush or a smile when he addressed her.

Itō said to the aged attendant:

'Many times, in my solitary walks, I have passed through this village without knowing of the existence of this honorable dwelling. And ever since entering here, I have been wondering why this noble household should have chosen so lonesome a place of sojourn . . . Now that your Himégimi-Sama and I have become pledged to each other, it seems to me a strange thing that I do not yet know the name of her august family.'

At this utterance, a shadow passed over the kindly face of the old woman; and the bride, who had yet hardly spoken, turned pale, and appeared to become painfully anxious. After some moments of silence, the aged woman responded:

'To keep our secret from you much longer would be difficult; and I think that, under any circumstances, you should be made aware of the facts, now that you are one of us. Know then, Sir Itō, that your bride is the daughter of Shigéhira-Kyō, the great and unfortunate San-mi Chüjō.'

At those words – 'Shigéhira-Kyō, San-mi Chüjō' – the young samurai felt a chill, as of ice, strike through all his veins. Shigéhira-Kyō, the great Heiké general and states-man, had been dust for centuries. And Itō suddenly understood that everything around him – the chamber and the lights and the banquet – was a dream of the past; that the forms before him were not people, but shadows of people dead.

But in another instant the icy chill had passed; and the charm returned, and seemed to deepen about him; and he felt no fear. Though his bride had come to him out of Yomi – out of the place of the Yellow Springs of Death – his heart had been wholly won. Who weds a ghost must become a ghost; yet he knew himself ready to die, not once, but many times, rather than betray by word or look one thought that might bring a shadow of pain to the brow of the beautiful illusion before him. Of the affection proffered he had no misgiving: the truth had been told him when any unloving purpose might better have been served by deception. But these thoughts and emotions passed in a flash, leaving him resolved to accept the strange situation as it had presented itself, and to act just as he would have done if chosen, in the years of Jü-ei, by Shigéhira's daughter.

'Ah, the pity of it!' he exclaimed; 'I have heard of the cruel fate of the august Lord Shigéhira.'

'Ay,' responded the aged woman, sobbing as she spoke; 'it was indeed a cruel fate. His horse, you know, was killed by an arrow, and fell upon him; and when he called for help, those who had lived upon his bounty deserted him in his need. Then he was taken prisoner, and sent to Kamakura, where they treated him shamefully, and at last put him to death.* His wife and child – this dear maid here – were then in hiding; for everywhere the Heiké were being sought out and killed. When the news of the Lord Shigéhira's death reached us, the pain proved too great for the mother to bear, so the child was left with no one to care for her but me – since her kindred had all perished or disappeared. She was only five years old. I had been her milk-nurse, and I did what I could for her. Year after year we wandered from place to place, traveling in pilgrim-garb . . . But these tales of grief are ill-timed,' exclaimed the nurse, wiping away her tears; 'pardon the foolish heart of an old woman who cannot forget the past. See! the little maid whom I fostered has now become a Himégimi-Sama indeed! – were we living in the good days of the Emperor Takakura, what a destiny might be reserved for her! However, she has obtained the husband whom she desired; that is the greatest happiness . . . But

---

* Shigéhira, after a brave fight in defense of the capital – then held by the Taïra (or Heiké) party – was surprised and routed by Yoshitsuné, leader of the Minamoto forces. A soldier named Iyénaga, who was a skilled archer, shot down Shigéhira's horse; and Shigéhira fell under the struggling animal. He cried to an attendant to bring another horse; but the man fled. Shigéhira was then captured by Iyénaga, and eventually given up to Yoritomo, head of the Minamoto clan, who caused him to be sent in a cage to Kamakura. There, after sundry humiliations, he was treated for a time with consideration – having been able, by a Chinese poem, to touch even the cruel heart of Yoritomo. But in the following year he was executed by request of the Buddhist priests of Nanto, against whom he had formerly waged war by order of Kiyomori.

the hour is late. The bridal chamber has been prepared; and I must now leave you to care for each other until morning.'

She rose, and sliding back the screens parting the guest-room from the adjoining chamber, ushered them to their sleeping apartment. Then, with many words of joy and congratulation, she withdrew; and Itō was left alone with his bride.

As they reposed together, Itō said:

'Tell me, my loved one, when was it that you first wished to have me for your husband?'

(For everything appeared so real that he had almost ceased to think of the illusion woven around him.)

She answered, in a voice like a dove's voice:

'My august lord and husband, it was at the temple of Ishiyama, where I went with my foster-mother, that I saw you for the first time. And because of seeing you, the world became changed to me from that hour and moment. But you do not remember, because our meeting was not in this, your present life: it was very, very long ago. Since that time you have passed through many deaths and births, and have had many comely bodies. But I have remained always that which you see me now: I could not obtain another body, nor enter into another state of existence, because of my great wish for you. My dear lord and husband, I have waited for you through many ages of men.'

And the bridegroom felt nowise afraid at hearing these strange words, but desired nothing more in life, or in all his lives to come, than to feel her arms about him, and to hear the caress of her voice.

But the pealing of a temple-bell proclaimed the coming of dawn. Birds began to twitter; a morning breeze set all the trees a-whispering. Suddenly the old nurse pushed apart the sliding-screens of the bridal-chamber, and exclaimed:

'My children, it is time to separate! By daylight you must not be together, even for an instant: that were fatal! You must bid each other good-bye.'

Without a word, Itō made ready to depart. He vaguely understood the warning uttered, and resigned himself wholly to destiny. His will belonged to him no more; he desired only to please his shadowy bride.

She placed in his hands a little *suzuri*, or ink-stone, curiously carved, and said:

'My young lord and husband is a scholar; therefore this small gift will probably not be despised by him. It is of strange fashion because it is old, having been augustly bestowed upon my father by the favor of the Emperor Takakura. For that reason only, I thought it to be a precious thing.'

Itō, in return, besought her to accept for a remembrance the *kōgai** of his sword, which were decorated with

---

* This was the name given to a pair of metal rods attached to a sword-sheath, and used like chop-sticks. They were sometimes exquisitely ornamented.

inlaid work of silver and gold, representing plum-flowers and nightingales.

Then the little *miya-dzukai* came to guide him through the garden, and his bride with her foster-mother accompanied him to the threshold.

As he turned at the foot of the steps to make his parting salute, the old woman said:

'We shall meet again the next Year of the Boar, at the same hour of the same day of the same month that you came here. This being the Year of the Tiger, you will have to wait ten years. But, for reasons which I must not say, we shall not be able to meet again in this place; we are going to the neighborhood of Kyōto, where the good Emperor Takakura and our fathers and many of our people are dwelling. All the Heiké will be rejoiced by your coming. We shall send a *kago** for you on the appointed day.'

Above the village the stars were burning as Itō passed the gate; but on reaching the open road he saw the dawn brightening beyond leagues of silent fields. In his bosom he carried the gift of his bride. The charm of her voice lingered in his ears – and nevertheless, had it not been for the memento which he touched with questioning fingers, he could have persuaded himself that the memories

* A kind of palanquin.

of the night were memories of sleep, and that his life still belonged to him.

But the certainty that he had doomed himself evoked no least regret: he was troubled only by the pain of separation, and the thought of the seasons that would have to pass before the illusion could be renewed for him. Ten years! – and every day of those years would seem how long! The mystery of the delay he could not hope to solve; the secret ways of the dead are known to the gods alone.

Often and often, in his solitary walks, Itō revisited the village at Kotobikiyama, vaguely hoping to obtain another glimpse of the past. But never again, by night or by day, was he able to find the rustic gate in the shadowed lane; never again could he perceive the figure of the little *miya-dzukai*, walking alone in the sunset-glow.

The village people, whom he questioned carefully, thought him bewitched. No person of rank, they said, had ever dwelt in the settlement; and there had never been, in the neighborhood, any such garden as he described. But there had once been a great Buddhist temple near the place of which he spoke; and some gravestones of the temple-cemetery were still to be seen. Itō discovered the monuments in the middle of a dense thicket. They were of an ancient Chinese form, and were covered with moss and lichens. The characters that had been cut upon them could no longer be deciphered.

*

Of his adventure Itō spoke to no one. But friends and kindred soon perceived a great change in his appearance and manner. Day by day he seemed to become more pale and thin, though physicians declared that he had no bodily ailment; he looked like a ghost, and moved like a shadow. Thoughtful and solitary he had always been, but now he appeared indifferent to everything which had formerly given him pleasure – even to those literary studies by means of which he might have hoped to win distinction. To his mother – who thought that marriage might quicken his former ambition, and revive his interest in life – he said that he had made a vow to marry no living woman. And the months dragged by.

At last came the Year of the Boar, and the season of autumn; but Itō could no longer take the solitary walks that he loved. He could not even rise from his bed. His life was ebbing, though none could divine the cause; and he slept so deeply and so long that his sleep was often mistaken for death.

Out of such a sleep he was startled, one bright evening, by the voice of a child; and he saw at his bedside the little *miya-dzukai* who had guided him, ten years before, to the gate of the vanished garden. She saluted him, and smiled, and said: 'I am bidden to tell you that you will be received to-night at Ōhara, near Kyōto, where the new home is, and that a *kago* has been sent for you.' Then she disappeared.

Itō knew that he was being summoned away from the light of the sun; but the message so rejoiced him that he found strength to sit up and call his mother. To her he then for the first time related the story of his bridal, and he showed her the ink-stone which had been given him. He asked that it should be placed in his coffin – and then he died.

The ink-stone was buried with him. But before the funeral ceremonies it was examined by experts, who said that it had been made in the period of *Jō-an* (1169 AD), and that it bore the seal-mark of an artist who had lived in the time of the Emperor Takakura.

Glossary

daimyō: The feudal lords of Japan, exercising great influence from the tenth to mid nineteenth centuries

Fudō: Deity of Japanese Esoteric Buddhism

harakiri: Form of Japanese ritual suicide by means of disembowelment, more commonly known as *seppuku*

hatamoto: Upper-rank samurai employed directly by the shōguns of feudal Japan

jinrikisha: Two-wheeled cart pulled by a man that usually functions as a small taxi

kaimyō: Name Japanese Buddhist monks and nuns are given when entering the religious life

kakémono: Japanese scroll painting

koto: Japanese stringed instrument

kuruma: Type of vehicle or cart; in Hearn's day the equivalent of a rickshaw or *jinrikisha*

kurumaya: The runner who pulled the *kuruma*

kwan: Coffin

Kwannon: Japanese goddess of mercy

Rokuro-Kubi: Japanese ghoul that takes human form and can either stretch its neck or detach its head, which can then move about independently

ryō: The currency unit used in Japan prior to the Meiji era

sen: A Japanese coin worth one-hundredth of a yen, the basic currency unit

yashiki: Residence or estate of a noble

yukata: Lightweight kimono, worn in the summer and traditionally made of indigo-dyed cotton

LITTLE CLOTHBOUND CLASSICS

Ryūnosuke Akutagawa · *Hell Screen* · 9780241573693

Elizabeth von Arnim · *The Enchanted April* · 9780241619742

Jane Austen · *Lady Susan* · 9780241582527

Karen Blixen · *Babette's Feast* · 9780241597286

Jorge Luis Borges · *The Library of Babel* · 9780241630860

Italo Calvino · *Cosmicomics* · 9780241573709

Albert Camus · *The Fall* · 9780241630778

Truman Capote · *Breakfast at Tiffany's* · 9780241597262

Anton Chekhov · *About Love* · 9780241619766

Kate Chopin · *The Awakening* · 9780241630785

Joseph Conrad · *The Lagoon* · 9780241619773

Fyodor Dostoyevsky · *White Nights* · 9780241619780

Arthur Conan Doyle · *The Adventure of the
   Blue Carbuncle* · 9780241597002

F. Scott Fitzgerald · *Babylon Revisited* · 9780241630839

Kahlil Gibran · *The Prophet* · 9780241573716

Lafcadio Hearn · *Of Ghosts and Goblins* · 9780241573723

O. Henry · *The Gift of the Magi* · 9780241597019

E. T. A. Hoffmann · *The Nutcracker* · 9780241597064

Shirley Jackson · *The Lottery* · 9780241590539

Franz Kafka · *Metamorphosis* · 9780241573730

Anna Kavan · *Ice* · 9780241597330

Yasunari Kawabata · *Snow Country* · 9780241597361

Nella Larsen · *Passing* · 9780241573747

Clarice Lispector · *The Imitation of the Rose* · 9780241630846

Katherine Mansfield · *Bliss* · 9780241619797

For rights reasons, not all titles available in the USA and Canada.